What if...

All the Boys Wanted You?

a choose
your destiny
NOVEL

What if...
All the Boys Wanted You?

LIZ RUCKDESCHEL AND SARA JAMES

DELACORTE PRESS

Published by Delacorte Press
an imprint of Random House Children's Books
a division of Random House, Inc.
New York

Delacorte Press and colophon are registered trademarks of
Random House, Inc.

www.randomhouse.com/teens

Educators and librarians, for a variety of teaching tools, visit us at
www.randomhouse.com/teachers

Library of Congress Cataloging-in-Publication Data
is available upon request.

ISBN-13: 978-0-385-73297-0 (tr.pbk.)—
ISBN-13: 978-0-385-90318-9 (glb)
ISBN-10: 0-385-73297-X (tr.pbk.)—ISBN-10: 0-385-90318-9 (glb)

Printed in the United States of America

10 9 8 7

First Edition

What if...
All the Boys Wanted You?

Father doesn't always
know best. . . .

"Who gave Mitchell chewing gum?" a still-groggy Haley asked. She had just woken up from a nap to find a sticky wad lodged in her long auburn hair.

Perry Miller looked at his daughter in the car's rearview mirror and shrugged. "He told me his ears were popping."

"I'll pop his ears," Haley muttered, pulling hard on the gum.

"Haley, don't. You'll just make it worse," her mother, Joan, said from the front seat.

"I have gum in my hair. How much worse can it get?"

Haley did sort of have a point. The impromptu Thanksgiving tour of New England in the Miller family station wagon hadn't exactly been a resounding success. The reason they were on the road again, not long after their cross-country move, was so that the kids could see Plymouth Rock and Perry could get extra footage for his next documentary on the life cycle of deciduous trees.

What the Millers hadn't counted on was the gridlocked traffic, the overbooked bed-and-breakfasts, or the local meteorologists being off, *way* off, on the weekend forecast. Instead of the brisk weather and blue skies they'd been promised, they were treated to a blustery nor'easter, with sheets of driving rain, sleet, and snow—not exactly ideal traveling conditions. And now, on top of everything, there was gum in Haley's hair.

"You did this on purpose," she said, glaring at her little brother as she tried to separate the wad into clumps.

Mitchell was always leaving roller skates in front of Haley's bedroom door or "accidentally" spilling the pepper shaker on her dinner.

"It was. Marcus," Mitchell said in his annoying robot voice.

"Don't try to blame your imaginary friend," Haley said as Freckles, the family dalmatian, whimpered and put a paw on her lap.

"He. Is not. Imaginary," Mitchell said.

"Just wait until we stop, Haley," her mother offered. "We might be able to get it out."

Haley couldn't believe what she was hearing. "So once again, Mitchell Miller gets away with murder," she said, rolling her eyes.

"I'm sure he didn't mean it," her mom said. "Did you, buddy?" Joan reached into the backseat and patted Mitchell's hand before turning on the radio and scanning the stations.

She was on a Beatles kick this trip. Meanwhile, Haley slumped down in the backseat, trying not to think about the gum—or anything else for that matter, but once her mom settled on the moody "Here, There and Everywhere," it was kind of hard not to think. *Could it really have been three months since we moved?* she wondered, thinking back on the last time they had all been packed in the car together.

Mitchell was still acting a little freakish, but he was the only member of the Miller clan who wasn't easily adjusting to their new life in Hillsdale, New Jersey.

Haley was even making a few friends and now recognized most of the faces in the halls at Hillsdale High. There was, for instance, the artistic Irene Chen, the clingy but nice Annie Armstrong, and the trio of populettes, Coco De Clerq, Whitney Klein and Sasha Lewis.

Even better, Haley had recently gotten chummy

with some of Hillsdale's biggest hotties. Such as . . . her neighbor Reese Highland, who was as comfortable in honors chemistry as he was on the soccer field. And Drew Napolitano, a jock who sometimes flirted with her in English class. Then there was Johnny Lane, the brooding frontman of the Hedon; his cocky friend Luke; Spencer Eton, Hillsdale's resident hedonist and SIGMA host, who usually could be found hanging out with his old boarding school roommate, Matt Graham; and of course, who could forget Sebastian Bodega, the Spanish exchange student who was only too willing to offer Haley lessons in the Romance languages? The biggest question mark for Haley, though, was Devon, an aloof photographer who went to art school in New York, but whom Haley occasionally bumped into in town.

Unfortunately, even the promise of a new boyfriend didn't keep Haley from occasionally feeling homesick for San Francisco, her old school and Gretchen, her best friend since the third grade. Most of all, Haley missed how simple her old life had been.

Now she had all these decisions to make—whom to sit with at lunch, which party invitations to accept, and what to do when someone passed her in the hallway without saying hello. It seemed as if everyone was always waiting to see if the new girl would make the right or wrong move.

That was why, when Haley's parents announced they were planning a Thanksgiving getaway, she found herself actually looking forward to five days away from Hillsdale, with no mean girls, no crushes, no boy trouble and definitely no drama.

But that was before the perfect storm had converged and Haley had woken up to a wad of Mitchell's gum in her hair. *What else can go wrong?* she wondered, staring cross-eyed at the pinkish knots.

Suddenly, the car engine sputtered. Perry eased off the gas and pulled to the side of the road.

"What is it?" Joan asked.

Freckles barked as the lights dimmed and flickered inside the car.

"That can't be good," Joan said.

Haley stared out at the cars zooming past them on the rain-slicked interstate. "Great," she said. "Now what am I supposed to do about my hair?"

Haley's mother had a worried look on her face. "Right now, Haley, I think that gum is the least of our problems."

An hour later, the Millers' station wagon was on a flatbed wrecker truck heading southeast to an auto dealership near the Massachusetts border.

"See, kids," their dad said, "I told you this would be an adventure."

"Marcus. Likes. Big trucks," said Mitchell.

"Haley. Hates. Big detours," Haley mocked.

When they arrived at the garage, Perry huddled with the mechanics while Joan made a few phone calls.

"Come on, Haley," she said after hanging up.

Haley frowned. "Where are we going?" she asked.

"There's a salon up the street," her mother said.

"W-wait. N-not so fast," Haley stammered, clutching her long hair protectively.

"Well, you said you wanted that gum out of your hair."

"What happened to seeing if we could comb it out?"

"What happened to you leaving it alone like I told you? Come on. They're only open till six."

Thirty minutes later, when the woman frantically cutting Haley's hair was finally finished, Joan said in an overly positive tone, "I think it suits you." Haley still refused to look at herself in the mirror. The five-inch locks of reddish brown hair scattered around the chair had already terrified her enough. "It's just a haircut, Haley," her mother added. "It'll grow back."

That, of course, was the worst thing she could have told Haley.

Back at the garage, Mitchell was sitting on the sidewalk, beaming.

"What are you smiling at, you little twerp?" Haley said. "I'm practically bald, thanks to you."

"Dad. Bought. A new car," Mitchell said.

"What!" Haley exclaimed.

And just then, Perry pulled up in a shiny new silver SUV.

"Anyone need a lift?" he asked, looking mischievously at his wife.

Haley was speechless.

Joan, on the other hand, had plenty to say. "If you think I'm riding one mile in that gas-guzzling, air-polluting road hog, then you're not the man I married."

"But Joanie, it's a hybrid," Perry said, a dumbstruck look on his face.

It took several hours of convincing, but once Haley's mom had carefully read and reread the paperwork and grilled two auto mechanics and three salesmen on the gas-and-electric vehicle's fuel efficiency, low emissions, and safety performance on the highway, she finally relented and said they could keep it—although Perry still felt the need to explain himself once they were back on the road.

"Just think how much safer you'll feel driving on the New Jersey roads this winter. You're not used to snow and ice."

Joan, still damp from the rain, shivered. "Here, do you want your seat heater on?" Perry asked, reaching toward the dashboard.

"No. I do not want my seat heater on," Joan said.

"I want. My seat. Heated," Mitchell said from the backseat.

Haley shushed him. She knew better than to get in the middle of one of her parents' "discussions."

"Come on, Joanie," said Perry. "You can't stay mad at me forever."

"What has our deal always been?" she asked.

"It was time for a new car."

"I was fine in the wagon. Now. What. Has our

deal. Always been," Joan repeated. Haley suddenly knew where Mitchell got his robot voice.

Perry mumbled, "No big purchases without consulting each other. I'm sorry. I should've talked to you first." He reached over and took her hand. "You have to admit, though," he added, "it is a pretty sweet ride."

Joan smiled.

"Look, there's even satellite radio," Perry said, pointing to the dial and showing her how to use it.

Haley breathed a sigh of relief. After the storm, the hair, and the roadside assistance, the last thing she wanted was to listen to her parents argue all the way back to New Jersey.

"Marcus is. Sorry. Too," Mitchell said to Haley. "He likes. Your new hair."

"Well, Marcus better learn to keep his gum in his mouth," Haley said. "Or the next time we take a family vacation, he's staying home."

"Affirmative," Mitchell said, snuggling up to Haley and Freckles for the long ride home.

Back in Hillsdale, Haley somehow managed to avoid looking at her haircut until Monday morning before school. When she could put it off no longer, she sat down in front of the mirror to assess the damage.

What she saw when she opened her eyes was . . . actually, not that bad. She hadn't morphed into a babyish tomboy, as she had feared. On the contrary, the layered, shoulder-length bob made her look . . . sophisticated, sexy, *older.*

Well, what do you know, she thought, smoothing out the ends and throwing on a chunky white sweater and jeans. *Mom was right. This haircut totally works.* Of course, Haley would never tell her mother that.

Downstairs, Joan was sitting at the kitchen table drinking her coffee and reading the newspaper. "Good morning," she said.

Haley, keeping up the act, remained silent as she poured herself a glass of juice.

"Are you still mad at me? I don't see why. You look great, like one of your father's students," Joan said, holding out Haley's packed lunch as Haley took a bite of wheat toast and gulped down the last of her juice.

"Does that mean I could pass for eighteen?" Haley asked, grabbing the brown bag.

Joan's face went white.

"Don't worry," Haley said. "Like you said, it'll grow back."

And with that, she slipped out the back door and hopped into the passenger seat of the new car next to Perry.

Haley's dad drove her to school and dropped her off in front of the main entrance. "Have a good day, honey," he said as she gave him a peck on the cheek and climbed out of the car.

A girl with long braids and a tie-dye T-shirt

glared at the SUV and shook her head. "You're the reason the country is addicted to oil," she said to Perry disapprovingly.

"But it's a hybrid," Perry said, giving Haley a helpless look.

"Don't worry, Dad," Haley whispered. "You know it's a hybrid, I know it's a hybrid and the planet knows it's a hybrid, and that's all that matters." She waved as he drove away.

Turning her attention to the courtyard, Haley saw that, as usual, Coco, Whitney, Spencer and their entourage were holding court with Annie and Dave Metzger hovering nearby. Sebastian was futilely trying to soak up some rays on the lawn, while Irene, Shaun and some kids from the Floods were congregating in the parking lot. Not far from them were Sasha, Johnny and the guys from the Hedon. Haley did a double take. Luke, it seemed, was actually in school for once. And for some reason Devon was also there. *Weird,* Haley thought. *And why is Sasha not hanging out with Coco and Whitney? And where the heck is Reese?*

In fact, her adorable neighbor was the one person Haley didn't see.

She took a deep breath and headed toward . . .

● ● ●

Fall is in full swing at Hillsdale High, and if you think Haley Miller's first few months at her new school were exciting, just wait until you find out what's in store for

her next. There will be sweet sixteen parties, holiday shopping trips, a California excursion and maybe even a game of strip poker, as Haley discovers the further benefits of being the new girl in school.

Spoiler alert: Haley Miller will soon have a boyfriend. But who will it be? Now that Haley has gotten to know most of the boys at Hillsdale, which one will she go after? And what if . . . they all come after her?

If you want to send Haley to THE COURTYARD to worship at the altar of the popular kids, turn to page 12. If you'd rather she veer toward the danger zone in THE PARKING LOT, turn to page 19.

When all the boys want you, life should be sweet. But is that what Haley Miller will find? It all depends on how you work, love and play with the girl with the most potential at Hillsdale High.

THE COURTYARD

Having a trust fund doesn't necessarily make you trustworthy.

Haley walked tentatively toward the courtyard, admiring Coco's and Whitney's impeccable clothes. Coco had on a cream knitted minidress with a chunky taupe belt and slouchy suede boots, while Whitney was in a tight pink sweater, a gray pencil skirt and pumps. *Why is it I never see them in the same thing twice?* Haley wondered.

They were chatting with Cecily Watson, a tall, dark-skinned cheerleader Haley had only recently gotten to know. Cecily had a funkier sense of style than Coco and Whitney and was wearing a preppy yellow oxford shirt, a camouflage miniskirt with a frayed hem and flat workboots.

Spencer Eton, whose blue collared shirt screamed white-collar parents, was entertaining a handful of jocks in varsity jackets. Haley noticed that Spencer's tan seemed improbably dark for late November. *So he either met his parents in the islands for Thanksgiving, or he's been hitting the local tanning salon again,* she thought. Knowing Spencer, it was probably a bit of both.

"Off," Coco demanded, brushing Spencer's hands away as he tried to rub her shoulders. "Don't handle the merchandise."

"What's wrong, De Clerq?" he asked. "Are you missing your new man?"

Coco acted as if she didn't hear him. Haley, meanwhile, fidgeted, adjusting her cowl-neck sweater until she felt a little less self-conscious about her new haircut. She was glad she had chosen to wear her tight jeans with her black high heels today. At least if her hair proved to be a disaster, she had on a cute outfit.

Whitney frowned and stared at Haley. "Paging Bob. New haircut alert," she said, elbowing Coco.

"Huh. There are hairdos, hairdon'ts, and hairdon't-even-think-about-its," said Coco.

"Hi, Haley," Cecily said, smiling at her. "Wow, your hair looks great. It's so shiny and healthy, you can tell you don't put any chemicals in it."

"What's that supposed to mean?" said Coco, frowning. It was widely known that Coco spent a fortune on her hair, tinting her mousy brown locks a spectrum of rich autumnal hues.

Cecily shrugged. "Sometimes I have my hair straightened, and it totally dries it out."

Whitney was self-consciously examining the split ends of her excessively highlighted mane.

"If you didn't use so much bleach, Klein, it might stop falling out in the shower," Coco said.

"Everybody's hair falls out in the shower," Whitney said defensively. "Doesn't it?"

"Sure," said Cecily, clearly trying to make her feel better.

Spencer turned his attention to Haley. "What a difference a weekend makes," he said. He let his eyes travel down Haley's curves.

"Leave her alone," said Coco.

"You jealous?" he asked.

"So where's Reese?" Haley said, glancing around.

Spencer looked annoyed. "You know, it's too bad Highland's asexual," he said. "He could be getting the best play in Bergen."

"Reese is not asexual," said Coco firmly.

"He's still in Europe with his family," Whitney explained to Haley.

Haley felt a knot in her stomach. *Are they dating now?* she wondered.

"The Highlands always travel during the holidays," said Cecily.

"He texted me all weekend while I was in Quogue," Coco bragged, picking up her vibrating cell phone. She looked down and read the screen, then looked up at Haley, smiling.

"Looks like the Highlands are touring Versailles today," Coco announced, adding, "Reese says hi, Whit."

"Hi, Reese," Whitney called out, as if he could hear her all the way from France.

Cecily frowned. "Since when did Reese get a satellite phone?" she asked.

"He didn't—" Coco said, suddenly realizing her mistake.

"D'oh!" said Spencer.

"Then how could he be sending you text messages from Europe?" Cecily asked.

"Did I say text?" Coco laughed it off. "He's been e-mailing me all week. I can check e-mail from my phone."

"Right," Haley said, looking at Cecily and smiling. There was, after all, nothing better than catching Coco in a lie. Especially when that lie had to do with Coco's ongoing attempts to snare Reese.

"So who wants to crash Senior Skip Day?" Coco asked abruptly.

"I'm in," Whitney said, collecting her book bag, which in actuality never carried any of her books. Who had room for textbooks when there were makeup bags, spare outfits and potato chips and cookies to cart around?

"Sure, why not," said Spencer. "The first day back after a holiday is always a wash."

"Speak for yourself. My geometry teacher's like a prison warden," said Cecily. "If I don't show, he doesn't even bother calling Principal Crum. He goes straight to my dad." She gathered up her things. "Until lunch, ladies."

"What about you?" Coco asked, eyeing Haley.

Just then, Annie Armstrong finally untangled herself from Dave and her newspaper long enough to notice that Haley Miller was in their midst. "Haley!" she exclaimed. "Great haircut. How was your break?" She handed Dave the crossword puzzle they'd been working on.

"I see someone has discovered a new four-letter word," said Whitney. "D-O-R-K."

"Are you sure it's not G-E-E-K?" Coco asked. "Or N-E-R-D?"

Haley looked at Annie and realized that for the first time since she'd met her, the popular girls weren't getting to her. Annie took Dave's hand and said, "We spent all weekend at a chess tournament in Connecticut."

Haley heard Spencer whisper to Coco, "That's not puppy love, dude. That's full-on doggie-style."

Sebastian wandered over, putting on his tie, which meant he was probably meeting with another college recruiter at lunch. Sebastian was already being courted by some of the best swimming programs in the country, even though he was only a sophomore exchange student from Seville.

"*Hola,* Haley," Sebastian said, leaning down to kiss her cheek. "*¿Cómo estás? ¡Qué guapa que estás hoy!*"

"*Estoy bien,* Sebastian. *Gracias.*"

"That's so weird," Whitney said. "It's like they have this secret little language."

"It's called Spanish, Whitney," said Coco. "We're in their class."

"Speaking of, time for Ms. Frick's," Annie said. "Are you coming, Haley?"

"*Sí,* Haley, *camine conmigo,*" Sebastian said. His voice, like his gaze, was hypnotic.

"Afraid not," Coco said, linking arms with Haley. "She's ditching with us. Right, Miller?"

"Haley wouldn't dare," Annie said.

"Get used to it, Headstrong," Spencer said, grabbing Haley's other arm. "She's one of us now."

Uh-oh. Here we go again, Haley thought, already worrying, once again, about making the right decision. Vacations, it seemed, were never long enough.

●　●　●

Once again, the social deck at Hillsdale High is being shuffled. Will Haley take the hand of the hot Latin Sebastian? Will she team up with Spencer, the king of the bluff? Or will she rebuff both their advances and wait for Reese Highland to come home from Europe?

Who would have thought that wannabe Annie

Armstrong would fall for the unpopular Dave Metzger? He's certainly not going to advance her position at Hillsdale. Let's just say she's putting body over mind in that decision. So will Dave's neurotic love finally make Annie sane? Or will Annie's girl-crush on Coco ultimately prove more powerful than her attraction to Dave?

And what about Coco? She seems pretty testy for having just had a vacation in Quogue with her family. Do you believe Reese e-mailed her from Europe? Or was she just lying to make Haley jealous?

For now, all Haley has to figure out is whether to head to SPANISH CLASS on page 33 with Annie, Dave and Sebastian, or SKIP SCHOOL on page 26 with Whitney, Coco and Spencer.

So what's more important, the risk or the reward?

THE PARKING LOT

Certain people always gravitate to the edge.

As Haley approached Shaun and Irene, she caught sight of the bright pink streaks that Irene had added to her hair over the break, and suddenly she stopped worrying about her own new haircut. *Guess losing a few inches doesn't really count as extreme,* Haley thought. *At least not around here.*

Devon was taking pictures of Garrett "the Troll" Noll ollieing on his skateboard and didn't notice Haley when she walked up. But she certainly noticed him. He was wearing his faded brown corduroys, gray skate shoes, and a blue sweatshirt, and with his golden head of mussed hair, he looked unusually cute.

"What's he doing here?" she asked Irene.

"Lost his scholarship to art school," said Irene.

"Bummer," Haley replied.

"Dude, you're thrashing," Shaun said as Garrett, dressed in all black with a white skullcap, popped his board up and slid along a railing at the edge of the parking lot.

"You catch that?" Garrett asked Devon as he skated by them on his board.

"Got it," Devon said, waving him on without looking up from his camera.

"Hey," Sasha said coolly to Haley. Haley returned the greeting, noticing the old jeans, holey sweater and black combat boots Sasha had on. Her once-beautiful long blond hair was a tangled mess, and there were dark circles under her eyes.

Johnny nodded hello to Haley and Irene. After a few days away, Haley had forgotten how truly gorgeous he was. Even with his slouch, his layered T-shirts and his five-day-old stubble, he looked great.

"Hey," Irene said to Johnny, without taking her eyes off Garrett. Haley could tell she was deliberately ignoring him, which only made her friend's crush that much more obvious.

"How was break?" Haley asked Irene.

"I spent four days serving rice and fried meat to lonely singles with no Thanksgiving plans of their own. How do you think it was?"

"Jump the steps, brother man," Shaun said to Garrett. He pointed to a series of concrete risers at the end of the parking lot. "Let's christen the Hillsdale Gap."

Garrett went to inspect the proposed jump, with Shaun, Luke and Devon in tow.

"What's he doing here?" Haley asked, motioning to Luke.

"Luke? He was ordered to start going to classes again," said Irene.

"By who, his mom?" Haley asked.

"His parole officer," said Irene. "His mom finally kicked him out of the house. He's couch surfing these days."

Luke ambled over to where they were sitting. "I liked you better with long hair," he said, running his fingers through Haley's hair.

"Subtle, Luke," said Irene.

He was hardly the type of guy Haley was normally attracted to, much less one her parents would approve of, but there was something compelling about Luke Lawson. Haley felt drawn to him, if only to see what kind of trouble he'd get into next.

"Like I had a choice," Haley said. "My little brother stuck gum in my hair."

"Want me to knock some sense into him?" Luke asked, all too seriously.

"Um, that's okay," said Haley. "He's six."

"Another typical fun-filled Miller family vacation," Irene said.

"Where do I begin?" said Haley. "The gum in my hair? The icy interstates? Or our car breaking down in the middle of New Hampshire?"

"Yeah, but you got a sweet new ride out of it, didn't you?" said Luke. "Speaking of, when can we take it out for a spin?"

"In about fifteen months, when I turn seventeen and get my driver's license," said Haley.

"I was surprised to see you pull up in that thing this morning. Aren't your parents a little green for an SUV?" Irene asked.

Haley shrugged. "It's a hybrid. Anyway, with my luck, next year my parents will move us to a state that doesn't allow unsupervised driving until age twenty. I'm cursed."

"At least you have parents," Sasha said absently. Haley suddenly felt guilty for complaining. She knew Sasha was having problems with her dad and that her mom was essentially out of the picture.

"This is why the Chens never go on vacation together," said Irene. "Too much togetherness and you want to poke each other's eyes out."

"But you spend loads of time with your parents at the restaurant," Haley reminded her.

"Yeah, you just proved my point," said Irene. "By the way, it's family night at the Golden Dynasty tonight. Come one, come all, and bring your dysfunctional gene pool."

"Hot diggity!" Shaun said, grabbing his stomach

as he approached. "Crab wontons, pot stickers, and sweet and sour pork. Now, that's what I call a happy family."

"I don't think I can make it," Sasha said, abruptly gathering up her things and accidentally spilling the contents of her backpack onto the asphalt.

Haley bent down to help her collect her belongings. Among the scattered pens, lipsticks, loose keys and packages of crackers lifted from the cafeteria was a wad of ten-dollar bills wrapped in a thick rubber band. Haley reached down to pick it up, but Sasha quickly snatched it away.

"Thanks," Sasha mumbled as Haley stood up and handed her a stray tube of lip gloss.

"No problem," Haley said, feeling awkward. She tried changing the subject. "So, you ready for the big soccer game next week?" she asked.

"I guess," said Sasha. "I haven't really thought about it."

"Come on, the best player on the team hasn't given a thought to the final game of the season?" Haley asked.

"Look, I gotta go," Sasha said, turning and heading toward the school building, but not by way of the main courtyard.

Something is seriously up, Haley thought.

"Hey, catch you guys later," Johnny said, taking off after Sasha. Irene tried not to seem too disappointed by Johnny's disappearance. *She is so not over him yet,* Haley thought, feeling sympathetic. She certainly knew what it was like to pine for someone who couldn't quite love you back.

Haley walked up to Devon, who was packing up his camera equipment. "I hear Hillsdale's sophomore class has a new member. If you want, I could show you around today," she offered. "I remember what it's like getting lost in the math wing."

"No thanks," said Devon. "I'll figure it out." He hoisted his bag over his shoulder and headed off to his first class.

So that's what I get for trying to be nice to him? Haley thought. *Let's see how he feels after geometry.*

"You can show *me* around," Luke whispered in Haley's ear.

Irene rolled her eyes. "Didn't you go here for, like, three years already, Luke?" she asked.

"Yeah, but a lot's changed since then," Luke said, picking up Haley's backpack. "Especially with regards to me."

"Yeah, like now you've got a rap sheet and a mustache," said Irene, picking up her own books and grabbing Haley's bag from Luke. "Come on," she said to Haley.

"See ya," Haley said to Luke.

● ● ●

Hillsdale's male student body's head count just went up by two. And you know what that means: two more sets of lips for Haley to potentially kiss.

So will Haley be able to help Devon make the best of his experience at Hillsdale High? Or will he continue to freeze her out?

Luke claims he's cleaned up his act, but should Haley believe him? What's it like to date a felon? And should Haley indulge her curiosity and find out?

As for Sasha, she's clearly hiding something. Just how much trouble is she in? Will Haley be able to help her? Or will Sasha's problems end up sucking Haley into her downward spiral too?

As usual, Haley must balance what's best for her and what's best for those around her. If you want her to look after Sasha and play in the last AWAY SOCCER GAME of the season, turn to page 41. If you think she should stick with Irene and take her up on the invitation to HAPPY FAMILY at the Golden Dynasty, turn to page 47.

There's a delicate line between avoiding trouble and turning your back on a friend in need. If Haley doesn't reach out to Sasha, who will? Then again, if she does, who's going to reach out to Haley?

There's a reason schools are called institutions.

"**S**hotgun," Coco said as her sister, Alison, pulled up in her convertible. Whitney and Spencer piled into the backseat, which meant Haley ended up on Spencer's lap.

"I love Senior Skip Day," Whitney said.

"Anything to get out of watching Ms. Frick flirt with Sebastian," Coco sighed.

As they pulled up to a stoplight, a dowdy woman in a minivan looked at them suspiciously. Haley didn't even need to turn her head to recognize Mrs.

Armstrong, Annie's mother, who worked at the same law firm as her mom.

If she catches me, I'm dead, Haley thought, snuggling up to Spencer to hide her face.

"Well, hi there," Spencer said, wrapping his arms around Haley's waist. "Tell Daddy Spencer all about it."

"Hey, not in my car. I just had the seats cleaned," Alison said sternly, eyeing them from the rearview mirror.

"Don't you mean our car?" Coco asked pointedly.

"That's right, the De Clerq sisters share everything," Alison said sarcastically.

"Ali, when I'm in your presence, I can't even think of another woman," said Spencer, lifting up his hands in surrender. Coco's shoulders tensed in the front seat.

"So where's Sasha been, anyway?" Ali asked, glaring at Haley, the interloper.

"Boy, do we have news," Whitney said, leaning into the front seat in between Ali and Coco.

"You mean all that stuff about her dad being a gambling addict, spending all their money in Atlantic City and disappearing?" Alison asked as the light turned green. "I heard that this morning, but I didn't believe it."

"It gets worse," Coco added. "Turns out, she's dating Johnny Lane."

Only Coco would think having Johnny Lane as a

boyfriend was worse than having a messed-up father, Haley thought.

"You're kidding," said Ali.

"Yeah. She's turned into a full-fledged parking lot freak," said Coco.

"So that's why you two are shopping for a new BFF. Personally, I liked Cecily better," Ali added. Haley frowned, suddenly liking Coco's sister less and less.

"Did you know Sasha's even quitting the soccer team?" said Whitney.

"Well, you have to give her some credit," Alison said, putting on an expensive pair of sunglasses. "Johnny Lane is kind of sexy."

"Sexy?" Coco said, horrified. "Don't you mean a dirty, useless, slum-dwelling, bottom-feeding mutant?"

"Honey, if Johnny Lane was hungry, I'd feed him any day of the week," Ali said, eyeing Spencer in the rearview mirror. Haley felt him shift beneath her on the seat. "Haven't you girls seen him onstage? Whatever 'it' is, he's got it."

"Spare me the 'guys make me weak when they pick up instruments' routine," said Spencer, clearly annoyed. "So he can strum a few power chords. Big deal."

"I think he's sort of cute," Haley said tentatively, enjoying a little the sight of Spencer scowling.

Coco rolled her eyes. "Miller, you're so getting tossed at the next light."

"See, I'm not the only one who's hot for the Hedon," said Ali.

Haley added, "I heard they're this close to a record deal." She held up her thumb and index finger and pushed them together until they were almost touching.

"Yeah, because I introduced them to a friend whose dad's in the industry," Spencer huffed. "Big mistake. They're no Rubber Dynamite." To console himself, he allowed himself a quick feel of Haley's thigh.

Minutes later, the car pulled up to Richie Huber's house, and Spencer leaped from the car, following Ali into the party, in the process nearly tossing Haley into the street. She tagged along behind Coco and Whitney.

Ali and Spencer seem awfully close for a senior and a sophomore, Haley thought suspiciously.

"Welcome," Richie said affectionately to the trio of girls, before frowning and adding, "Where's Sasha?"

How many times am I going to hear that today? Haley wondered.

"Nice to see you too, Richie," Coco said, pushing by him and walking straight to the kitchen, wedging herself in between Ali and Spencer. She poured herself a glass of orange juice without mixing in any champagne.

"Too early for champers?" Whitney asked.

"Yeah, by like seven weeks," said Spencer. He turned to Haley and said, "Coco drinks only once a year, on New Year's Eve."

Ali poured herself a glass of champagne without mixing in any juice. "My sister's uptight," she said, looking at Haley.

"It's just empty calories," said Coco, defending herself.

"They're not empty, baby," said Spencer as Ali poured him a glass of champagne. "They're packed with fun." He squeezed Haley around the waist, said, "Be right back," and followed Ali upstairs.

Whitney, meanwhile, was diving into an array of bagels, lox and gourmet cream cheeses. "Oooh, I love locks! Hey, why do you think they call it that, anyway? And who has the key?"

"Klein, watch the carbs," Coco snapped.

"It's cool you have a sister to drive you everywhere," Haley said. "I'd kill for that kind of freedom."

"Well, there is a downside," said Whitney.

"What do you mean?" Haley asked.

Coco glared at Whitney, but as usual, Whitney didn't get the hint to shut up in time. "It means, how would you feel if every time you brought a guy around, your older sister ended up sleeping with him?"

"Whitney!" Coco said, trying to silence her.

"Wow. That's harsh," said Haley. "But I still say it's worth it. I can't believe you have to wait until you're seventeen to get a license in New Jersey. It almost makes me want to move back out West."

Coco looked momentarily out of sorts before

regaining her composure. "So, Haley. What are you up to Friday night?" she asked.

"Not sure yet. Why?"

"I say we have a sleepover," said Coco.

"Okay," said Haley, wondering what had provoked the sudden surge of friendliness in Coco.

"At your house," Coco said. "I want to see what life is like *chez* Miller."

How typical, Haley thought. *I find out something damaging about Coco, and now she needs to even the score by digging up dirt where I live.*

"I don't know. I'll have to ask my mom," she said.

"Oh, wait a minute. That's right. Whitney and I already told Cecily we'd do something with her this weekend."

Unbelievable, Haley thought. *She really is trying to play Cecily and me off each other. Well, I know how to solve this.* "Why don't we just invite Cecily to my house too?" she said.

"If you're sure it's all right," Coco said innocently.

"What's this I hear about a slumber party?" Richie asked, putting his octopus arms around Coco and Haley. "And where's my invite?"

"Don't you wish?" Coco teased. "He'd like nothing more than to spend the whole night watching us have pillow fights in our underwear."

After forming the mental image in his head, Richie clutched his heart and keeled over dramatically. Coco made it a point to step right on his chest as she left the room, with Whitney trailing right behind her, devouring another bagel with cream cheese.

● ● ●

So what's up with Spencer Eton and Coco's big sister? Is there really something going on between them? Or is Spencer just going after Ali to make Coco, or maybe even Haley, jealous?

Coco and Whitney certainly seem to have found their replacement candidates for Sasha Lewis. Should Haley be flattered or offended that she and Cecily Watson are in a runoff election to become Coco and Whitney's new BFF?

And what about Sasha? It's one thing to gossip about her downward spiral, but has anyone bothered to check on her lately?

To stop by the Lewis apartment after school, turn to CHECK ON SASHA on page 73. To have Coco, Whitney and Cecily come to the Millers' for a sleepover on Friday night, turn to SLUMBER PARTY on page 55. Finally, if you think Coco is too fickle and manipulative to be a friend to Haley, send Haley on a SHOPPING SPREE with her mom instead on page 63.

So what did Haley miss by skipping out on a day of school? That's the thing—you'll never, ever know.

SPANISH CLASS

Over three hundred million people in the world speak Spanish. Not among them: Whitney Klein and Coco De Clerq.

Annie sighed and said, "Of course, Ms. Frick forgets to take attendance the day Coco, Whitney and Sasha cut class."

Uh-oh, Haley thought. *Here comes another Armstrong rant.*

Haley braced herself for a barrage of complaints about the Coquettes. Instead, a miraculous thing happened. Dave put his hand on Annie's arm, and as he did, Annie relaxed.

"You know what," she said, gazing back at Dave. "Who cares if Coco never gets into trouble? I'm here, with my real friends, learning Spanish. Heck, maybe I'll even get to study abroad in Spain someday. Coco's only punishing herself."

Haley couldn't quite believe her ears. Was this the same Annie Armstrong she'd met only three months ago? The Annie who used to keep a detailed account of Coco's infractions, which she read aloud at every available opportunity? Dave really did seem to be mellowing her out.

"*Hola,* class!" Ms. Frick said as she sashayed up to the front of the room. "Who wants to tell me about their Thanksgiving?" she said, eyeing Sebastian.

"*Rrrrroxanna,*" Ms. Frick said, turning her attention to a tiny girl with tawny skin and glasses who was avoiding eye contact at the back of the room.

Roxanna? Haley thought, not recognizing the girl's Spanish name. "Who is that?" she whispered to Annie.

"That is Hannah Moss," Annie said, tightening her grip on Dave's arm.

Hannah was small for her age—okay, make that teeny-tiny—and when she stood up to respond to Ms. Frick, Haley realized Hannah was wearing the same green corduroy overalls Haley had once owned. In the fourth grade.

Ouch, Haley thought. *She's stuck in 6X.*

Haley listened as Roxanna/Hannah recounted her vacation in passable Spanish. Haley quickly realized that the only thing Hannah had done over fall break was work on her computer. Make that build her computer. Hannah had evidently taken parts from a few corrupted hard drives, an old TV and an instrument keyboard panel, and created a machine she called "El Frankenstein."

Wow, Haley thought. From the look on Dave's face, he was equally impressed, a development that unfortunately didn't escape Annie's attention.

"Bien, Roxanna," the teacher said, calling next on the drowsy Drew Napolitano. *"Juan, dígame."*

Drew rubbed his eyes. "Uhh . . . I went fly-fishing with my dad in Argentina. We even spoke some Spanish. It was wicked awesome," he said, nodding back off.

"Ah, Argentina," Ms. Frick cooed, pulling down a South America map from above the blackboard. She spent the next five minutes talking about the region's agriculture, topography and city life before retracting the map and writing on the blackboard in her flowery penmanship, *Group Projects: The visual presentation of your city.*

"Sebastian," she said, batting her eyelashes, "tell us, what will your group bring in to represent your assignment, Seville?"

"Let me think," Sebastian said, basking in the spotlight. "I do not know if there is a way to do this, Ms. Frick."

"Whatever do you mean, Sebastian?" Ms. Frick responded coyly.

"Well, how do you re-create a sunset?" he asked. "What can I show you that will take you to the markets on a busy morning? A picture cannot work, not even a painting by a Spaniard like Picasso."

"Then what do you propose?" Ms. Frick asked, leaning against her desk.

He stared at her intently. "You will all have to close your eyes and listen while I take you on a walking tour of the city. You will hear the sounds. You will smell the smells. And then in your mind's eye, you will see the city that I call home."

"Very good, Sebastian. Very good indeed. You have such an elegant speaking voice, it will be a pleasure, won't it, class, to listen to your every word." She smiled seductively. "For the other groups, those of you who do not have such personal connections to your cities, I expect you to bring in objects or visual aids that are unique to your region and its traditions. Now please assemble in your groups to discuss. Chop-chop."

Dave turned around, clearly happy to be looking directly into Annie's eyes again, while Sebastian and Haley moved their desks to join them.

"Haley," Sebastian said, leaning across his desk to get a better look at her. "It is as if last week, you are a girl, and today you are a woman. I did not know a simple haircut could make such a difference."

"Really?" she replied, self-consciously tucking a loose strand behind her ear. She was flattered by Sebastian Bodega's attention. He was, after all, Sebastian. It was just that sometimes he could be, well, a little too much.

"Okay, amigos." Annie took the floor. "Sebastian has already offered to give us an auditory walking tour of his hometown. I think we should come up with ways of enhancing the presentation. Sebastian, perhaps you can make a list of sounds and smells someone would encounter as they made their way through the city? Church bells, trains, the fresh bread of a bakery. I also propose we enlist the art teacher, Mr. Von, to help us re-create the experience. I heard he spent a year in Seville in the eighties."

"Really?" Haley asked. "Doing what?" Everyone at Hillsdale knew that Mr. Von was legendary.

"He was a flamenco dancer," said Annie.

"As it happens," Dave said, "I'm interviewing Mr. Von on my podcast this weekend. We can ask him then."

"Sure," said Haley, leaning back in her seat and putting her feet up. With Dave, Annie and Sebastian around, she barely had to do any work.

"Ahem," a timid voice interrupted. Haley turned around and saw that it was the wee'un, Hannah Moss.

"What do you want?" Annie frowned.

"Did I hear you guys say you needed to re-create certain sounds?" Hannah asked.

"It's for Sebastian's virtual walking tour," Dave said, with a friendly, welcoming look on his face.

"Well, I'm great with a synthesizer," Hannah offered. "I mean, if you need any help."

"Cool." Dave smiled and nodded at her.

"No offense, Hannah," said Annie, "but why

would you want to take on extra work? Don't you have your own group to worry about?" Haley couldn't believe Annie was being so rude.

"Actually," Hannah said, "I was out sick on the first day of school, and the second, and the third."

"But you're feeling better now, though, right?" Dave asked, concerned.

"Allergies," Hannah explained with a shrug.

"You too?" Dave asked, whipping out his inhaler.

"That ragweed's a killer," said Hannah. "When I finally started classes, Ms. Frick assigned me to work with Coco and her group, but they wouldn't let me join. And I've been sort of afraid to say anything ever since. I certainly don't want to get Coco in trouble. If you know what I mean."

"Well, we already have four people," Annie said sharply. Dave frowned at her.

"Annie," Haley whispered. "Don't you think you're being a little, um, harsh?"

"What's this," Ms. Frick said, approaching their group. "Why are there five of you here?"

"Ms. Frick," said Sebastian, piling on the charm. "Roxanna, she is just what we need for our group. She wishes to help us, but is afraid you will not let her. I told her you are a wise and generous woman and would have no problem with this arrangement. Might she be allowed to join us?"

"Well," Ms. Frick began, "it's not exactly fair to the other students."

"You can grade us on a curve," Dave offered.

"Dave!" Annie shouted, looking at him as if what he'd said was sacrilege.

"It's okay," said Hannah. "I'll just do a presentation on my own."

"No, no, that wouldn't be fair either," said Ms. Frick. "I guess I'll allow you to work on Seville with the others." Dave and Hannah smiled at each other. "But I must warn you," she added, "I will be expecting extra-special things from this group."

Annie folded her arms across her chest and huffed. And for the first time since Haley had joined her gifted Spanish group, she felt there was the slightest possibility that she might not be in for such an easy A after all.

● ● ●

With so many overachieving type-A personalities in Haley's Spanish group, they should be on A+ cruise control. But will personal problems start getting in the way of their grades?

Just when Annie and Dave's relationship seemed to be blossoming, Hannah Moss has arrived. So will the Moss grow on Dave? Or will Annie get her guy in the end? And how will this love triangle affect Haley's day-to-day?

Speaking of guys, is Sebastian the right one for Haley? Should she be falling for someone who's going back to Spain in, oh, six and a half months?

If you think it's fine for Haley to pair up with the brainiacs during school hours, but want her to socialize with a different crowd in her spare time, send her on a SHOPPING SPREE with her mom on page 63. If you think Haley should stay close to her group, lest she suffer brain shrinkage by associating with normal types, send her to the Metzgers' house for MR. VON'S PODCAST on page 67.

Haley's a smart girl, but being smart doesn't necessarily mean she has to go geek. The trick is figuring out how to balance all her gifts—not just her brains, but also her beauty and her wicked sense of humor.

AWAY SOCCER GAME

There's no ace like home—as in home field advantage.

Haley climbed onto the activity bus and walked down the aisle, saying hi to her teammates as she looked for an open seat. "Miller, have you seen Sasha?" Coach Tygert asked her.

"Um, I thought she'd already be here," Haley said, with a sinking feeling in her gut. She sat down next to a senior, Padma, and overheard one of the girls muttering, "She's not coming. She no-showed at practice this week."

It was true Sasha had been threatening to quit the

team, but Haley had never imagined she'd be able to skip the last games of the regular season.

"Hey," Haley said, while stowing her bag under the seat. "So no word from Sasha at all?" Padma shook her head.

Padma's family was from Mumbai, India. She had skin the color of coffee with cream, amber eyes, and long wavy hair that was so black it was almost blue. And she was good on the field. So good, in fact, that Haley had at first been intimidated by her. But the senior had watched out for the sophomore, and now they were friends.

Coach Tygert waited exactly ten minutes. And then, with only a flicker of disappointment on his face, he boarded the bus and said, "Okay, Willy. Let's move 'em out." He took his seat in the first row, looking over his playbook.

The girls were silent as they eased through the parking lot. Haley kept looking out the window, searching for Sasha. *Maybe she's just late,* she thought, even though it was clear Sasha had let them all down.

This wasn't just the last game of the regular season. And it wasn't just against Ridgewood, Hillsdale's chief rival. The two teams were tied for first place in the division. If the Hawks won, they would move on to the playoffs, and the seniors on the team, like Padma, might actually have a shot at taking home a division title before they left for college at the end of the year.

Without Sasha on the field, however, the Hawks didn't stand a chance.

"Got a problem here, Coach," Willy said, slowing down and pointing ahead to an intersection a few blocks from the school.

Haley looked out the window. Another yellow activity bus was on the side of the road with smoke streaming from under its hood.

"I bet that's the boys' team," Coach Tygert said. "What do you think, Willy, do we have room for a few more?"

"Bring 'em on," Willy said, pulling over.

"Great," said Padma, shutting her A.P. chemistry book. "There goes our concentration."

The guys filed onto the bus, nudging one another into the empty seats, with some of them fighting to claim spots next to certain girls.

Haley was surprised to see Reese Highland at the end of the aisle. Here she was in her baggy soccer shorts, shin guards and cleats, with her hair pulled back in a ponytail—not exactly her best look—and he was headed straight for her.

"Hey, Red," Reese said when he got to Haley's row. She and Padma slid closer to the window so that Reese could squeeze onto the edge of their seat.

"You're back" was all Haley could manage. She'd heard that the Highlands had gone to Europe for fall break, which was why Reese had missed school the previous week.

"We got in late last night," he said. "Couldn't

miss the last game of the season. But man, am I jet-lagged. I just hope I don't get confused and score for the other team." He dropped his bulky gym bag onto the floor of the bus near his feet and closed his eyes.

"Maybe we should put you in a Ridgewood uniform, just to be safe," Haley teased.

Reese opened one eye and looked at her playfully. "You think you're funny, Miller?"

"Well, at least one of our teams should win today," Haley said.

"You're worried," Reese said. Haley nodded. "Don't be. I'm sure you'll do great. You've been coming along all season."

"Tell that to the butterflies."

At that moment, Reese's stomach growled. "Do your butterflies want to meet my hungry grumblies? I'd kill for one of those chocolate croissants from Paris right now. Sasha's mom took us to the best bakeries."

"Wait, you saw Sasha's mom in Paris?" Haley asked, shocked.

"I didn't even know Sasha had a mom," Padma said. "I mean, at least not one who was still alive."

"Messy divorce," said Reese. "Her mom moved back to Europe. And Sasha, well, you know how she can be. She sort of held a grudge."

"So how did you find her?"

"My parents have kept in touch with her. Sasha's mom and my mom went to the Sorbonne together for undergrad. In fact, Mrs. Lewis met Mr. Lewis at my parents' wedding." He looked over his shoulder toward the back of the bus. "The story's hilarious. Where's Sasha? She tells it better than I do."

Haley shrugged. "Dunno."

Reese looked surprised. "But Sasha's never missed a game against Ridgewood."

"Yeah, well, Sasha's been pulling a lot of firsts lately," Padma said.

"You know her mom asked me how she was doing. I wish I'd known something was up."

"I don't think Sasha's really in a place to accept help from anyone right now," said Haley. "Certainly not her mom."

A few minutes later, the bus pulled into the Ridgewood parking lot, and the teams went to meet their fates. Reese walked with Haley as far as the locker rooms.

"Good luck out there today," he said as Haley tried not to get psyched out by the hordes of home team fans, the banners, the painted faces, the parents carrying bullhorns and pom-poms.

"We don't need luck," she said, jogging to catch up with Padma and the rest of her team. "We need Sasha." Then she yelled back to him, "Or a miracle."

● ● ●

So Sasha Lewis's mother is alive and well after all. The question is, is Sasha? Under normal circumstances, Sasha would never let her team down by missing a game, much less the last game of the season. But clearly, these aren't

normal circumstances. So should Haley be worried about her friend?

As for Reese, he's certainly acting interested in Haley. Is he secretly pining for her as much as she's pining for him? Or is Haley doomed to "just be friends" with her cute crush from next door?

If you think Haley should go CHECK ON SASHA, turn to page 73. To have Haley stick closer to home, send her on a SHOPPING SPREE with her mom on page 63.

As for the Lady Hawks? They lost to Ridgewood, 12 to 2. Unfortunately, Sasha's self-destruction didn't affect only her.

**There are six words for
family in the Chinese
language. And Irene Chen
knows none of them.**

As the Millers pulled up to the valet parking in front
of the Golden Dynasty, a wilted head of lettuce came
flying from the bushes at their shiny new SUV.

"Pig!" they heard someone yell in a thick Chinese
accent. "Road hog!"

"But it's a hybrid!" Perry yelled through his open
window. "It gets thirty-one city miles to the gallon!"
This time, a head of red cabbage came through the
window and landed in Joan's lap.

"That's just Lonnie," Haley said, spotting the

Golden Dynasty's dishwasher lurking near the Dumpsters.

"And why is Lonnie throwing rotten vegetables at our car?" Joan asked, raising an eyebrow at Perry, as she rolled down her window and dumped the cabbage into a trash can. "Or should I say our piggish, road-hogging American SUV."

"Lonnie's way into the environment," Haley explained. "Irene told me he sends all his money back home to China to fight unethical development and natural resource depletion. I think you'd like him, Mom. You should hear what he has to say about the Three George Dam."

"You mean the Three Gorges?" her mother asked.

"That's what I said." Haley rolled her eyes.

As Haley got out of the car, her mother looked at her layered T-shirts, torn jeans and old mismatched sneakers and said, "Haley, we really need to take you shopping."

"I dress like this because I want to, Mom," she said. "Not because I don't have anything else to wear."

"Still, you could use a winter coat," said Joan. "And some new shoes."

"Welcome, welcome!" Mr. Chen beamed at the Millers as they walked through the double doors. "Right this way," he said, leading them into the main dining room.

Irene was, as usual, standing behind the black marble counter at the hostess station.

"I told you we'd make it," Haley said.

"Hi, I'm Joan," Haley's mom said with a smile, extending a hand to Irene. "Haley's told us so much about you. Were those your murals out front?"

"Mom . . ." Haley shushed her.

"Yeah," said Irene. "You'd never know there were child labor laws in this country, would you?" She forced a smile and glanced at her father.

"Well, she's certainly got spunk," Joan whispered to Perry as Mr. Chen rattled off something to Irene in Chinese.

"Come on. I reserved a table by the pond for you guys," Irene said, leading them past the long buffet. "It's a flat fee tonight, all you can eat, kids under twelve are free. Plates are on the table. Drinks are at the bar. And trust me, do yourselves a favor and stay away from the moo shu pork. It's a little heavy on the pepper tonight."

"But no MSG, right?" Perry asked.

"Uh-oh," Haley said, knowing exactly what was coming.

Irene paused, maintaining her cool. "Actually, Mr. Miller, that whole MSG thing? It's a myth. MSG, or monosodium glutamate, is just a heightened form of the naturally occurring amino acid glutamic acid, which has been used for centuries as a flavor enhancer and is found in abundance in foods like tomatoes and parmesan. That's why shaker cheese and ketchup make almost everything they touch taste so good."

Haley cringed. "Only a very small percentage of the population is, in fact, allergic to MSG," Irene continued, "as studies have shown, and even then, only fasting subjects given massive doses in liquid form reacted. But, in answer to your question, no, we don't add synthetic MSG, or as they call it in China, where it's made from fermented molasses, gourmet powder, to the dishes on our menu. Mostly because of certain . . . misinformed hypochondriacs."

"Wow," said Perry. "You really know your stuff."

"There is some naturally occurring free glutamate in the Golden Dynasty's food. And if that upsets your obviously highly sensitized digestive system, Mr. Miller," Irene added for effect, "I wholeheartedly apologize. But my suspicion is, you will have an excellent and episode-free meal."

Perry managed a smile. "Thanks."

"Enjoy," Irene replied, heading back to the hostess station. "Come find me in a minute," she whispered to Haley.

Joan was smirking at her husband. "So all that pouting you do after you eat Chinese? 'Joanie, I feel sick. Joanie, rub my neck.' That's all . . . what? Psychological?"

Perry, clearly looking for a distraction, ruffled Mitchell's hair and pointed to the pond. "Hey, buddy, look at the koi." He held Mitchell by his T-shirt so that he could lean toward the pond and get a better look at the goldfish.

"I'll be right back," Haley said to her mom. She

located Irene on the other side of the restaurant seating Whitney Klein, her father and soon-to-be-stepmonster in a corner booth.

"Ugh, I'm starving. Family night's the best," Whitney said, before eyeing Trisha. "Well, at least the food part of it anyway."

"I can't believe you two dragged me here." Trish whined as Mr. Klein squirted his mouth with breath spray. "This does not qualify as 'out to eat.' "

"Oh, right," Whitney said. "I always forget you're the restaurant expert. Seeing as you used to work in one."

"You little brat!" Trish took a swipe at her from across the table.

"It's like I've got two kids," Mr. Klein said to Irene as he tried to separate them. "How's about we stop bickering, act like young ladies and hit the buffet?"

Irene grabbed Haley's arm and backed slowly away from the table, sensing that the situation was about to erupt. Sure enough, as soon as Whitney and Trish reached the buffet, they started throwing wontons at each other.

"So how come you haven't asked me about California yet?" Irene said.

"I don't know. I just thought you'd bring it up when the time was right."

Haley was still feeling guilty for secretly submitting Irene's drawing to *Mission* magazine. Sure, Irene had won the contest—along with two round-trip tickets to San Francisco. But she hadn't exactly been thrilled about the unauthorized entry. Haley had nearly bungled their new friendship, and even though Irene eventually forgave her, Haley wasn't about to pressure her into handing over one of the plane tickets.

"Well, I'm bringing it up now," Irene said, pulling something from her back pocket. "I can't go without a tour guide." She held out the ticket.

"Are you sure?" Haley asked, hesitating.

"Yes, I'm sure. If I try to punish you, I'll just be punishing myself. There's no one I'd rather take."

"Really? What about him?" Haley asked, motioning to Shaun, who had just entered the Dynasty with his mom and dad.

"Haven't you heard?" Irene said. "Shaun's parents have a board meeting at the San Francisco MOMA that week, and they're bringing Shaun and Devon. We'll all be out there together. Except, Devon doesn't know yet. He's been acting sort of weird about invitations ever since his scholarship was rescinded."

"Yeah, I've noticed," said Haley. She looked over at the attractive couple standing next to Shaun. "So *those* are Shaun's parents?" she gasped.

"Yep."

Shaun's dad was wearing a charcoal gray suit and had a full head of silver hair, while Shaun's mother, a striking brunette, was in a narrow black dress with tall boots. "They're so thin. And . . . shiny," Haley said, staring at the beautiful, beaming couple, who so clearly doted on Shaun.

"What, you thought Shaun was raised by wolves?"

Haley paused. "More like overweight bears. In a cave full of banana sandwiches," she said.

"We can talk about the trip later," Irene said. "Just start working on your parents now so you can go."

"Okay," Haley said, unable to believe her luck. *A week in San Francisco with Irene, Shaun and Devon? Plus I get to see Gretchen and all my old friends from San Francisco? This is turning into the best year ever.*

Back at the Millers' table, Haley sat down with a full plate and an impish look on her face.

"What's gotten into you?" her mother asked while spooning some of her shrimp dumplings onto Mitchell's plate.

"It's just that I was talking to Irene the other day, about California—" Haley began.

Perry interjected, "I don't know if I like you hanging around this Irene person. She seems to have a lot of attitude, if you ask me."

"Oh, please," said Joan. "In fact, I think we should have her over to the house for dinner. Say, next week. Now, what were you saying, Haley, before your father so rudely interrupted you?"

"Oh, nothing," Haley said, diving into her sesame chicken. As long as her dad was anti-Irene, she didn't have much chance of getting both her parents to agree to the trip. "Nothing at all," she added, knowing full well she'd have to start working on her mom first. Now all she needed was a plan.

● ● ●

Wow, does Haley ever have her work cut out for her. How in the world is she going to convince her parents to let her go to San Francisco with Irene and the boys, when her father thinks Irene's a bad influence?

If you think it's a lost cause for Haley to even try to get permission, send her on that SHOPPING SPREE with her mom on page 63. Otherwise, go to PLAN THE TRIP with Irene on page 80.

The prize is never won by the person who drops out of the race. Then again, Haley entered this competition illegally, by submitting Irene's drawing without her friend's permission, so does she really even deserve that ticket to California?

Slumber parties were never intended for sleeping.

Alison De Clerq dropped Coco, Cecily and Whitney off in front of Haley's house with enough luggage to stay for a week.

Haley's first thought was *What have I gotten myself into?* "Welcome to Casa Miller," she called out from the front porch with a wave.

"Casa Miller?" Whitney whispered to Coco. "More like Cottage Miller, if you ask me." In a louder voice, she added, "It's so . . . cute."

"I know, right? Like a little doll's house," Coco agreed, inspecting the property as she teetered up the walkway in high heels, dragging her designer totes behind her.

"Hi, Haley." Cecily beamed, putting Haley at ease. "Thanks so much for having us."

Coco and Whitney took turns air-kissing Haley before dropping their bags on the porch and plopping down on the swing.

"Hot chocolate?" Haley asked, lifting a thermal pitcher. "Sugar's a rarity in this house, so drink up. I had to put in a special request."

"Are your parents health fanatics? Mine too," Cecily said. "If it's not organic, it doesn't come through the Watson front door."

"And here I thought we were the only green family in New Jersey," said Haley.

"There are a few of us, wedged in between all the smokestacks and shopping malls," said Cecily.

Whitney lunged at the first full mug of hot chocolate, but Coco threw out an arm to stop her. "Just a smidge for us, thanks," Coco said.

Cecily topped hers off with a homemade marshmallow as Haley poured smaller amounts into Coco's and Whitney's cups.

"So what's on the agenda for tonight?" Coco asked.

"Well, my mom's cooking a big dinner," Haley began. "Chicken and dumplings."

"I thought we'd order pizza," Coco countered. "Without the cheese."

"Um, okay," Haley said.

"What else?"

"We can watch movies in the basement," Haley offered.

"Only if we invite the boys over. Your parents won't mind," Coco said matter-of-factly.

"I don't know," Haley said. "They approved a sleepover. They didn't approve a boy-girl house party."

"Leave that to me," said Coco.

"I'm bored." Whitney was admiring her manicured nails.

"Want to go hang out in my room?" Haley asked, realizing it was going to be a very long twenty-four hours with the Coquettes in the house.

Coco breezed past the bags on the porch and right into the living room as Whitney instinctively jumped up and followed her. Haley and Cecily, of course, were left behind to deal with the bags.

"You guys really put the *lug* in *luggage*," Cecily said, dropping their stuff next to the staircase. "Great house," she added, admiring the simple white walls, the wooden cupboards and the family photographs scattered throughout the living room.

"How . . . quaint," Coco said, proceeding on her self-guided tour.

The girls entered the kitchen, where Haley's mom was sitting at the table helping Mitchell with his homework.

"Intruder alert," Mitchell said. "Intruder alert. Marcus. Has. A ray gun."

Cecily played along, holding up her arms. "Don't shoot," she said. "We're unarmed."

"Guess the short bus stops here," Whitney whispered to Coco, just loudly enough so that everyone in the room could hear her.

"Girls, I'm Joan," Haley's mom said, forcing a smile.

"Hello, Mrs. Miller," Coco replied frostily.

"You have a beautiful home," Cecily said. "I love your kitchen." Her smile was warm and sincere.

"Huh. Nice fridge," Whitney said, looking at the brand-new silver appliance. "We have one just like it in our garage."

Haley suddenly understood the look on her mother's face. It said, *Cecily, I like. But if either of those other two spoiled brats makes one more offensive comment in my house, this little slumber party is over, you got it?*

"Let's go upstairs," Haley suggested, hoping to head off disaster.

Along the way, they passed Haley's dad in his study, where Freckles was napping at his feet. "Hi, girls," Perry said without looking up from his stack of reference books. "I'd get up and come meet you, but by the looks of those bags at the bottom of the stairs, you'll be staying awhile. So no rush."

"Thanks for having us, Mr. Miller," Cecily said politely.

"Yes. Thanks, Mr. Miller," said Coco. She seemed impressed by Perry's chilly reception, which didn't exactly surprise Haley. After all, the only thing Coco ever responded to was a show of force. As they continued down the hall, Coco turned to Haley, linked arms with her and said, "I think it's so cool your father's a professor."

"I know," Whitney chimed in. "And can we talk about how much of a babe he is?"

"So not what I needed to hear," Haley said, opening the door to her room.

"Wow," said Whitney. "It's, like, smaller than my closet."

"Don't worry. There are sofa beds set up in the basement. We'll sleep down there," Haley explained.

"Not a bad view, though," Coco said, looking at Reese's bedroom through Haley's window. Whitney took out her digital camera and used the zoom lens.

"I can even make out the pattern in his comforter." Whitney giggled. "This is going to be so naughty and fun."

"Just wait till Spencer gets here," said Coco.

"Spencer Eton? Coming here?" Haley asked. "When?"

"Chill out. He and some of the guys are sleeping at Reese's tonight. Well, not exactly sleeping. You see, after your parents go to sleep . . ."

"I hate to break it to you, Coco, but my dad is a night owl. He sometimes stays up until after midnight reading. And even when he does go to bed, he's a really light sleeper. There's no way he won't hear us if boys are in the house."

"So the party starts a little later than expected. Big deal," said Coco.

"What did you think, we were going to sit around and paint our toenails all night?" Whitney scoffed.

"Why don't we just play it by ear?" Cecily offered. "If it seems too risky, we'll abort mission."

"I just don't want to ruin my holiday season by getting in trouble three weeks before Christmas," Haley said, more to herself than anyone else.

"Hey, did you guys hear that someone raided the cafeteria after school again yesterday?" Cecily said. "They took like five hundred dollars."

"Poor Whit. Daddy cut off your credit cards again?" Coco teased. "You know I can always lend you the cash."

"Very funny," Whitney said. "Seriously, who do you think did it? I bet it was one of those guys from the Floods. Like that Leprechaun one. He had a brand-new leather jacket on the other day."

"You mean the Troll?" Cecily asked.

"Yeah." Whitney shivered. "He's so creepy. Why do you think they call him the Troll?"

"That's just Garrett," said Cecily. "He's harmless. He works for my dad at the nursery. Which is how he got the money for that jacket."

"You know who I think did it," said Coco.

"Who?" asked Whitney.

"Sasha."

"No way!" Whitney gasped.

"She's totally broke now that her dad's gone postal. I hear he even gambled away her college fund."

"Nuh-uh," said Whitney.

"Wouldn't you steal if you had no money to live on, your dad had disappeared and your reputation was already in shambles? I mean, it's like the natural next step."

"No way," said Cecily. "Sasha would never steal. Not knowingly anyway."

"I agree with Cecily," said Haley. "Sasha may be going through a rough time, but she'd work in a cafeteria before she'd steal from one."

"Is that so?" Coco asked. "And how do you both know Sasha so well? We're the ones who've been friends with her since birth."

So why aren't you sticking up for her? Haley wanted to say.

"They're here," Whitney squealed, running to the window. Haley looked out and saw Richie Huber's car rolling up the Highlands' driveway with Spencer in the front passenger seat and Drew Napolitano and Matt Graham in the back. "Let the games begin."

"But which game is it going to be, Haley?" Coco asked. "Would you rather play truth? Or dare?"

● ● ●

Haley's mom didn't seem at all impressed by the De Clerq–Klein introductions. And who could blame her? Haley seems to be working awfully hard to fit in, but is she prepared to pay the dues required by the popular clique?

And what about Cecily? She's clearly a better

person than Coco and Whitney combined, so why is she hanging out with the Coquettes? Is everyone at Hillsdale ultimately susceptible to Coco's will? And if Cecily can't escape it, will Haley be able to?

You heard Coco. Truth? Or dare? To seek out the truth about the mysterious THEFT IN THE CAFETERIA, turn to page 93. Or turn to page 87 if you want Haley to TAKE THE DARE and sneak the boys into the house.

Normally, the prospect of a late-night basement session with Reese Highland would be enough to drive Haley to at least bend the rules. But with Coco, Whitney and Cecily around, will Reese pay any attention to Haley? Or will she get stuck fending off Richie Huber's octopus arms? And more importantly, should Haley trust Coco when her curfew and her parents' faith in her is at stake?

SHOPPING SPREE

Sometimes, the question isn't to be or not to be. It's to buy or not to buy.

By the time Haley had reached age fifteen, she had come to accept the fact that her mother wasn't like other moms.

For instance, her mom always had at least one symbolic pin or colored ribbon pinned to her natural-fiber lapel. When Haley brought friends over after school, instead of baking chocolate chip cookies, Joan made granola. Haley's mom didn't rent the latest movies from the local video store. She left out DVDs highlighting the plight of Native Americans, or deforestation in Madagascar, for Haley and her friends to watch. This, shall we say, didn't exactly enhance Haley's popularity with the kids at school.

Which is not to say that Haley wasn't proud of her mom. She looked up to her for sticking by her beliefs and actually trying to make the world—and now New Jersey—a better place. It was just that sometimes, Haley didn't know where the cause ended and her mother began.

But she was always surprised by the rare invitation to do something with her mom that didn't involve marches, Mitchell or Perry. Today, the request was even more unusual, since the mother-daughter activity Joan had picked was shopping for new winter coats.

Joan wasn't what you would call a born shopper. In fact, she was a vocal opponent of the so-called capitalist machine. But after seeing Haley's daily uniform of old jeans and T-shirts, Joan was ready to do the unthinkable. She was ready to take Haley to the mall.

"Are you sure you're up for this?" Haley asked tentatively as they got out of the car and looked up at the mammoth, windowless concrete structure in front of them. If the store logos had been stripped away, Haley decided, it could've been a prison. Or a fallout shelter.

"I'm ready," Joan said, steeling herself for the onslaught of bad lighting and mood music.

"Okay, let's go," said Haley, leading her mom through the main entrance and into what could only have been described as an explosion of Christmas past, present and future.

There were giant candy canes lining the walls, and four-foot snowflakes suspended from the ceiling. Two dozen or so college students dressed in elfin garb were leading small, screaming children up to "Santaland" to have their photo taken with St. Nick himself. Then there was the giant "Giving Tree" bearing the names and ages of needy kids who would go without Christmas if not for the kindness of strangers. A smallish train set wound its way around the base of the tree, and a wax-figure conductor occasionally pulled a mechanical cord, causing the engine to let out a loud *woowoo*.

The whole festive scene was, of course, covered in a light dusting of fake snow.

"Tell me why we're here again," Joan suddenly blurted out.

"Coats," said Haley, mesmerized by the glittery fabulousness of it all. "We need coats."

After one pass on the upper level, Haley had found a stylish knee-length black wool coat, a gray cashmere sweater, a pair of dark denim jeans and some brown corduroys. With their primary mission accomplished, her mother said they could stop in one more store before choosing four names off the Giving Tree—one for each member of the Miller family—and heading home for the day.

In one of the funkier boutiques, Haley spotted a purple beaded and appliquéd top that looked like something Whitney Klein would wear. There was a preppy tweed skirt that Haley could see on Annie Armstrong. She found a pair of brown suede moccasin boots with fringe that were very cool, though she thought only someone like Sasha Lewis could get away with them. And finally, there was an all-purpose black hoodie that for some reason reminded Haley of Irene Chen.

"You can choose one," her mother said, looking at the four items Haley had selected to try on. "And then I think you're done shopping for the next decade."

Haley looked at the pile, wondering which one would suit her best, and then disappeared into the dressing room to find out.

● ● ●

If you want Haley to buy the purple top, send her to SIGMA (page 120). For the skirt, send her to CHEZ VON (page 102). The moccasin boots, send her to THEFT IN THE CAFETERIA (page 93). And the black hooded sweatshirt, PLAN THE TRIP (page 80).

MR. VON'S PODCAST

The pod people
have spoken.

"That's an interesting point, David," Mr. Von said softly as he leaned closer to the mike. "Sometimes it does feel like I've lived nine lives."

Hillsdale High's eccentric art teacher, Rick Von, was in Dave Metzger's living room being interviewed for Dave's podcast, "Inside Hillsdale."

"And which one was your favorite?" Dave asked, scanning his blue note cards for his next question.

Mr. Von hesitated. "Well, Dave," he said poignantly in his throaty voice. "It's always the one I'm living right now."

Haley, Annie, Sebastian and Hannah Moss were smushed together on the Metzgers' mustard yellow sofa, trying not to giggle or cough or whisper too loudly as Mr. Von answered "Inside Hillsdale"'s version of the infamous Proust questionnaire. Dave had, after all, been nice enough to move his equipment out of his tiny bedroom so that Annie and the others could sit in on the live stream.

But every few minutes, Sebastian would reach out and squeeze Haley's knee or tickle her waist, trying to provoke an outburst. Then Haley would retaliate by blowing in Sebastian's ear or stealing his cell phone from his pocket. All the while, Annie and Hannah gave them disappointed looks from either end of the sofa.

Unfortunately for Dave, even without factoring in his classmates' antics, the interview hadn't exactly been going well. Dave had the most mysterious and interesting faculty member at Hillsdale High captive. Here was finally an opportunity to sort through all the rumors that had been swirling about Mr. Von since he had arrived in New Jersey two years ago. But, as Mr. Von had said during the first five minutes of the podcast, "Truth is relative, David. It all depends on your narrator."

Twenty minutes in, just as Dave had been about to make his first real breakthrough about Mr. Von's birth mother and the family that had adopted him, the loud roar of a vacuum cleaner in the next room had disrupted the mood. Dave had been able to convince his mom to postpone her dust-busting session. But Mr. Von never quite got comfortable again.

"We're here live with nomad, art teacher, philosopher, and cult hero of Hillsdale High Rick Von. Or, as some of you may know him, Acid Rick, the Von Time Trap, Rick Von Wrinkle—"

"Thank you for sharing those monikers with me, David," Mr. Von said, his voice barely above a whisper. "I didn't know the students had such clever nicknames for me. Sometimes I wish they would channel more of that creative energy into their painting."

Dave cleared his throat. "So, as you were saying. You were born in . . ."

"I guess I feel reborn whenever I move. So in a way, Hillsdale is my birthplace."

Dave looked deflated. "Mr. Von. From herding goats above Waimea in the sixties, to the salmon canneries of Alaska in the seventies, to the dairy farms of Tasmania in the eighties, you've sampled many professions and many cultures. And yet you're still alone. A bachelor. Living in a three-bedroom ranch house in Hillsdale Heights."

Mrs. Metzger, who had taken a seat in the den to observe, looked intrigued. "Tell me," Dave continued, "has there ever been a lady friend in your life?"

Dave's mother leaned forward, waiting for Mr. Von's response. Mr. Von took off his glasses and wiped the lenses. "I think I'll save that story for another program, Dave. It's been lovely being here."

"Well, that's apparently all the time we have for

this week's podcast, folks. I hope you enjoyed that somewhat murky glimpse inside Hillsdale's favorite journeyman, Rick Von. Now, a brief note to all you listeners out there. If anyone knows anything about the cafeteria theft last week, please, don't be an accessory to a crime by not speaking up. Principal Crum has had security cameras installed around campus, so it's only a matter of time before the culprit is caught. So do everyone a favor. Tell us what you know. Before someone tattles on you. You can file a report anonymously on my Web site. This has been Dave Metzger for 'Inside Hillsdale.' Thank you for listening." He switched off his microphone and stopped the feed.

Mrs. Metzger began clapping enthusiastically. "Brilliant, just brilliant. Hello, I'm Dave's mom, Nora," she said, extending her hand.

"Hello," Mr. Von said as their eyes met. Haley imagined a cheesy overture playing and the two of them running in slow motion through a field of daisies until they collided in an embrace.

Sebastian turned to her, pulling her out of her somewhat unsettling daydream. "I have to go to swim practice, but I must see you alone. Soon," he said. Haley felt a rush. She didn't know if she was ready to be alone with Sebastian just yet. Everything about him was so over-intense, she had a feeling that a date with him would qualify as a wedding night in some cultures.

"Just call me later," she said as he kissed her goodbye on the cheek. She looked at her watch and realized it was almost time to get going and pick her brother up from his therapy session.

"Mr. Von," Annie said, interrupting his moment with Mrs. Metzger. "We were hoping to talk to you about this project we're working on for our Spanish class."

"Why don't you kids come by my studio this week," Mr. Von said to Annie. Then he looked at Mrs. Metzger and added, "Perhaps, Nora, you could find the time to bring them?"

Mrs. Metzger blushed. "Of course," she said, nervously fiddling with the hem of her apron. She turned to Hannah, whose inhaler was peeking out of the chest pocket of her green overalls. "And who are you?" Mrs. Metzger asked, leaning down to Hannah's eye level and pinching her cheek.

"I'm in Dave's Spanish group," Hannah said.

"You're in high school?" Mrs. Metzger asked, confused.

"This is Hannah, Mom," Dave said. "The girl I was telling you about."

Annie looked crushed. Haley guessed she had never gotten an introduction like that.

"I love your smock, Mrs. Metzger," Hannah added.

"Well, aren't you sweet," Mrs. Metzger said. "You can call me Nora, dear."

As Hannah continued to bond with Mrs. Metzger

and Dave over food allergies and the merits of utility clothing, and Annie's depression visibly set in, Haley had an eerie feeling that the fabric of their cozy little Spanish group was beginning to tear.

● ● ●

So is Hannah Moss destined to come between the perfect couple, Dave and Annie? Will Haley and Sebastian go too far if Haley keeps spending time with him? And what will happen between Mrs. Metzger and Mr. Von?

To find the answers to all these questions and more, send Haley to Mr. Von's studio in CHEZ VON (page 102). If you think this path will only lead to unsolvable problems for Haley, send her to investigate that THEFT IN THE CAFETERIA Dave mentioned, on page 93. Or have her pick up her little brother at therapy, and possibly catch a glimpse of her cute neighbor, Reese Highland, in THE MILLER HOUSEHOLD on page 109.

Flirting with someone from another culture is one thing. But actually dating a foreigner? It's not quite as easy as falling for the cute boy next door.

CHECK ON SASHA

A world without parents is a world you don't want to see.

Haley was supposed to pick up Mitchell from his therapy session at four and watch him until supper, but she needed to find out what was going on with Sasha first. It was unlike her friend to skip school and a big soccer game and not return phone calls. Haley was getting worried.

She figured there was just enough time to swing by the Lewis condo before she picked up Mitchell, since it was technically on the way.

Little did she know what she would find when she got there.

Outside the front door of the apartment, a pile of *Bergen County Register*s sat, still in their plastic sleeves. Haley noticed that a few of the papers were at least two weeks old. *That can't be good,* she thought, ringing the doorbell.

"Sasha?" she called out, knocking when no one answered. "Mr. Lewis?" She turned the knob and was surprised to find the door unlocked.

Haley's first reaction when she entered the apartment was that it had been ransacked. The normally neat, modern space was in shambles. Chairs were overturned. Electronics equipment was missing. There were muddy boot prints on white area rugs.

Haley was about to dial 911 on her cell phone when she spotted something peculiar: a pair of electric guitars plugged into the living room wall. A cluster of take-out containers, empty liquor bottles and two ashtrays overflowing with cigarette butts on the coffee table confirmed her suspicions.

Looks like the work of the Hedon, Haley thought. The room was straight out of a rock documentary— the part where the group unravels and somebody winds up facedown in a pool.

"Sash?" Haley said, tiptoeing through the apartment.

Haley heard voices in the kitchen but found it was only the television. An overly serious anchorwoman announced, "Tonight, a story about a string of thefts at a local high school. What you need to know if your child is a student at Hillsdale High."

Weird, Haley thought. *She must be talking about the cafeteria robberies.* Principal Crum had just put out an all points bulletin notifying students that the school was once again on turquoise alert.

Haley found a stack of unopened mail in the kitchen. Several of the envelopes were stamped with bold red "past due" warnings, and on some of the return labels, Haley recognized the names of two New Jersey attorneys, Scott Winkler and Bob Balboa.

Coincidentally, a Balboa and Winkler ad appeared on the TV.

"Have you been injured on the job or in a vehicular accident that wasn't your fault? Did you trust the wrong medical professional, and suffer the scars to prove it? Are you trying to track down a deadbeat dad or adopt a child from a third world country? Then call Balboa and Winkler. Attorneys you can trust." Scott Winkler then winked for the camera as their catchy jingle played: "New Jersey law, it's on your side!"

At that moment, Haley heard the front door slam.

"Who's boozing?" Luke bellowed, entering the kitchen and making his way to the fridge to grab a beer. He didn't notice Haley, but when Johnny and Sasha entered a few seconds later, Sasha immediately spotted her.

"What are you doing here?" Sasha demanded. Haley could tell she'd been drinking.

"No one answered the door when I knocked," Haley said. "You weren't in school today. I was worried something might have happened."

"Something did happen," said Sasha. "The maid quit." Luke laughed.

"Where's your father?" Haley asked.

"My best guess would be Atlantic City," Sasha said. "He'll turn up. Eventually."

"Do you need a place to stay? Or money?" Haley asked.

"Sweet of you to offer," said Sasha, "but Luke already paid the electric bill. And as you can see, we've got groceries. Why don't you just go back to the land of the white picket fences where you belong?"

"She's just trying to help," Johnny said as Sasha breezed by him and went into the living room. Johnny followed her, and Haley could hear them quietly arguing in the next room.

"You got a real philanthropic streak," Luke said to Haley, turning on the gas burner and lighting a cigarette. He blew smoke rings that hovered in the air above her head.

Haley couldn't help feeling just the slightest bit attracted to him.

The clock on the wall read 3:45. *Just enough time to walk to the therapist's office and get Mitchell,* she thought. *But then what do I do about Sasha?*

Haley knew if she kept quiet, her friend's situation would just get worse. But if she told anyone about Sasha's predicament, Sasha might end up in the custody of Child Services, and that didn't seem like an appealing option either.

And then there was Luke. Hot, sweaty, sexy Luke, who was now rubbing Haley's shoulders.

"Relax," he said. "You're so tense." Haley closed her eyes. She wished she could forget about everything that was troubling her, Sasha and Mitchell included, and just give in to temptation. *How bad could it be?* she wondered.

● ● ●

To leave Haley ALONE WITH LUKE, turn to page 99. If you think Haley should leave the Lewis condo immediately, keep reading.

● ● ●

"Look," Haley said, breaking free of his grasp. "I just wanted to see for myself if Sasha was okay, and clearly, she's . . . not about to die or anything." In fact, Sasha and Johnny were, at that moment, feverishly making out in the living room.

"Whatever," said Luke, snuffing out his cigarette and throwing his hands up in the air.

"I'll see you around," Haley said before hurrying out of the apartment.

It was just under a mile to the therapist's office, and if she walked fast, she'd barely make it.

About a quarter of a mile down the road, Alison De Clerq drove by with Coco and Whitney in the car, stopped and pulled up to Haley in reverse.

"Miller, what are you doing in this part of town?" Coco asked.

"Checking on Sasha," Haley said without breaking her stride. "I thought someone should, seeing as her friends have all abandoned her." Ali kept the car rolling slowly alongside her.

"Oh, we've been up to the Hedon's little love nest," said Coco.

"I had to take, like, ten showers afterwards," Whitney said. "That guy Luke is a walking disease."

"Really?" Ali said absently. "I think he's sort of hot."

"Well, shouldn't we do something for her?" Haley said.

"Really now, did it look like Sasha wanted your help?" Coco asked.

Whitney added, "The only assistance she's interested in is mouth-to-mouth from Johnny Lane."

"Is this going to take long? I thought we were going to pick up Spencer," Alison said, checking her lipstick in the rearview mirror.

"Forget Sasha," Coco said to Haley. "She's a lost cause. Besides, there are more important things to think about."

"Like what?" Haley asked.

"Like Spencer's hosting a private SIGMA this weekend," Whitney announced.

"And you're invited," said Coco. "He specifically asked us to bring you." Ali glared at her sister. "Come on," Coco said to Haley. "We'll give you a lift."

She opened the door, staring at Haley, almost daring her to refuse.

＊　＊　＊

So what's it going to be? Should Haley keep trying to help Sasha, even though it's clear Sasha doesn't want her around? What would happen if Haley told her parents about Sasha's living situation? Remember those thefts at school the newscaster mentioned? Could Sasha be so desperate for money she'd resort to robbing the cafeteria? And if Sasha didn't do it, who did? Finally, there's Coco and Whitney's offer to consider. Should Haley forget about Sasha's problems for a while and double down with the cool kids? Are Whitney and Coco the sort of friends Haley needs?

You choose. To have Haley look into the THEFT IN THE CAFETERIA, go to page 93. If you think Haley should head home with Mitchell to regroup, turn to THE MILLER HOUSEHOLD (page 109). Or hang with the in crowd at SIGMA on page 120.

Sasha technically isn't Haley's responsibility, but if Haley does nothing and something happens to Sasha, will she be able to forgive herself?

Fools rush in. Idiots stall and wait to see what will happen.

"Chinatown's all about Grant Avenue," Haley said, wearing her new black hooded sweatshirt and sitting in the lotus position on the beige area rug in her living room. She and Irene Chen were planning their upcoming trip to Haley's old hometown, San Francisco.

"Isn't that sort of touristy?" Irene objected, hovering over the map they'd spread out on the floor. "I like that sweatshirt, by the way." Irene pointed to the intersection of Sacramento and Stockton. "This is where my parents want me to go. Kill-it-yourself live markets, dim sum, and—"

"The Chinese railroad workers mural?" Haley said.

"You've seen it?" Irene asked.

Haley cleared her throat and, in her best tour guide voice, said, "With only hand tools at their disposal, these immigrants laid ten miles of track in twenty-four hours." She shrugged and added, "Class trip, three years in a row."

"Whatever, I still have to check it out," said Irene. "My great-aunt lives somewhere around there."

Haley kept flipping. "Oooh, what about the Golden Gate Fortune Cookie factory?" she said, pointing to one of the dog-eared pages of her parents' Bay Area guidebook. "It says you can actually watch the fortunes being put into the cookies."

"We'll add it to the list," Irene said, jotting it down in her black sketchbook. Moments later, there was a knock at the front door.

"Dlohesouh relliM eht siht si? Ereh evil yelaH seod?" Shaun asked through the door, disguising his voice in a high falsetto.

"What's up, boys," Haley said, opening the door to welcome Shaun and Devon into her home.

"Hey," Devon said sheepishly.

Shaun brushed by Haley, immediately launching into a riff on the eighties pop song "Your Love" by the Outfield. "Irene's on a vacation far away. Hitting San Francisco with her friends. And there's so much I want to say. Yeah, you know I like my girls a little bit bolder." He came up behind Irene and played a dramatic solo on his air guitar.

"Promise me, Shaun. No more singing after we leave for the airport?" said Irene.

"Whatever, hoss. Minute we get to that hotel, you're getting a lap dance."

"I'm trembling with anticipation," Irene said flatly.

"You chicks hear about the latest boost at school?" asked Shaun. "Cafeteria got lit up again, five hundred bucks."

"I bet it's a lunch lady," Irene said. "Fanny Pincus so does not belong on the payroll of the New Jersey public school system."

"Really?" Haley said. "You don't think it's a student?"

Devon suddenly seemed anxious. "Sweet house," he said, changing the subject and gravitating toward the cinematography and film criticism books stacked on the living room shelves.

Shaun took the lid off his forty-eight-ounce cup of soda. "Yo, Haley, you gots any marshmallows? I need some floaters for my root beer."

"Gross," said Irene, articulating the sentiments of everyone in the room.

"Sadly, you've just entered a sugar-free zone, Shaun," said Haley. "Marshmallows require a written request at least two days in advance."

Shaun reached into the dish of mixed nuts on the coffee table and dropped a handful into his cup. "These'll do," he said, crunching on his soda.

"Dude, that is sick," Devon marveled.

Irene kept studying the map. "I can't believe we're all actually going on this trip," she said.

"Yeah, thanks to Shaun's parents," Devon replied, somewhat uncomfortably.

Irene looked up at him. "So how did Shaun finally convince you to take the ticket?"

"He drew two comic strips. One showed what my weekend would be like if I stayed in Hillsdale. And the other showed us in San Francisco, hitting Third and Army, Pier Seven and this secret skate park in the Presidio. It was impossible to refuse."

"We're talking epic," said Shaun. "This weekend will go down in the history of all histories."

Yeah, Haley thought. *If my parents let me go.*

Haley had been waiting for the right moment to ask Joan for permission. But her mother's caseload at the law firm kept her at the office late every night for weeks, so there had been few opportunities to sit down and talk through it. And this was definitely something that would need to be talked through.

Haley suddenly realized that if marshmallows required a written request two days in advance, San Francisco was going to take a dissertation. Submitted yesterday. *Why do I always procrastinate?* she wondered.

"You put the pygmy forest on that list yet?" Shaun asked, sucking on a soggy pecan. "It's supposed to be bizz-zarr-row. Like out of a Godzilla movie or something, only you're the monster." He began clumsily stomping pillows on the floor.

"I assume you're talking about the Mendocino dwarf trees?" Haley asked, stunned to discover another living, breathing human being interested in a topic her father had talked about almost daily in San Francisco.

"Is it like a bonsai garden?" Devon asked.

"Nope. Freak natural occurrence," Haley said.

"Just like the Shaun," Irene said.

"You know it," he said, nodding and smiling. "Heck yeah. Lilliputian anomaly." He belched loudly. "While you cats are on the Alcatraz ferryboat, munchin' on clam chowder and sourdough, I'll be stomping short stacks out in the forest."

"It would be kind of cool to play around with scale on my next photography project," Devon added.

"Seert nikhcnum eht gnoma uoy rof esop ll'yelaH ebyam," Shaun said in a babyish voice.

"*Au naturel,* of course," Irene added. Haley suddenly realized that Irene had learned to speak Shaun. *Weird,* she thought.

"Hi, kids," Haley's mom said, entering through the front door with Mitchell by her side. Her arms were full of brown grocery bags, and her purse and keys were dangling from her fingertips.

"Let me get that for you," Devon said, jumping up and promptly lightening Joan's load.

"Thanks," she said. "My, what a gentleman."

"Mom, Devon," Haley said casually. "Devon, Mom."

"Nice to meet you, Mrs. Miller."

"Irene you know," Haley said. "And this . . . is Shaun."

"We're the geniuses going on the Cali trip with young Haley," Shaun blurted out.

Joan stood there, looking confused.

"You know? Irene's trip? The one she won for getting published in the *Mission*?" Shaun explained. Haley's face turned bright red.

Irene stared at her friend, dumbfounded. Her face said it all: *How could you have not asked your mom to go on a three-thousand-mile trip that we're supposed to be leaving for in, oh, three days?*

"Haley, may I have a word with you in the kitchen?" Joan said swiftly.

Uh-oh, Haley thought. *This is not how this was supposed to play out.*

● ● ●

Looks like Shaun might have just inadvertently blown the trip for Haley.

To have her begin begging and groveling to see if she can convince her parents to let her go, turn to PLEASE, PLEASE, PLEASE (page 113). If you think Haley has a better shot at going if she tells her mother she'll stay with her old friend Gretchen, turn to STAY WITH GRETCHEN on page 115. To opt out of the trip entirely, send Haley to figure out what's going on at school in THEFT IN THE CAFETERIA (page 93).

All is not lost. Haley can still end up on the West Coast. However, you might not want to have her pack her bags just yet.

TAKE THE DARE

Sometimes it pays to play it safe.

The girls followed Haley downstairs to the basement, where Haley's mom had set up two sofa beds with blankets and clean sheets. On one side of the spacious room, there was a viewing area with an old color TV set, a VCR and a stack of VHS tapes. On the opposite side, there was a kitchenette, an old Ping-Pong table that Haley's dad had recently found at a yard sale, and a shelf with a turntable and records.

"Wow," Whitney said. "It's, like, prehistoric down here."

Cecily began flipping through the record collection.

"Will your parents mind if we play something?" she asked.

"Go ahead," Haley said. "Actually, I think they'd be thrilled if one of my friends got their music."

A loud knock at the back door startled Haley, but it was only the pizza deliveryman. She paid him the money her dad had given her and took the two warm boxes over to the Ping-Pong table.

"Okay, we've got one double cheese with pepperoni . . . ," Haley said, handing Cecily the box. "And one plain pizza, light sauce, no cheese."

Whitney glanced longingly at the pepperoni pie, but Coco shook her head and instead handed her half a slice of the cheeseless, fat-free stuff. Coco had recently imposed a diet on Whitney, since she said the bingeing was causing her to balloon up. Meanwhile, Haley poured regular ginger ale for Cecily and herself, and sparkling water for Coco and Whitney. "Sorry we don't have any diet soda," Haley said. "My mom thinks they're full of carcinogens."

"I mixed diet soda and gin once," Whitney said, taking a bite of her plain pie. "Let's just say it wasn't a good experience."

"Haley," her dad called from the top of the steps, "did you get your pizza?"

"We did, Dad. Thanks," Haley called out.

"Yes, thank you, Mr. Miller," Coco chimed in. "It's delicious."

"No it's not," Whitney whined. "The only reason to eat pizza is for the cheese."

"So who's the Hendrix fan?" Perry called out.

"That would be Cecily," said Haley.

"You've got a great vinyl collection, Mr. Miller," Cecily called up. "My father would be so jealous."

"Haley, did you show her those early LPs by the Band?"

"No, Dad. Not yet," Haley yelled back.

"Well, if you need me, I'll be in my office."

"Thank you, Mr. Miller," said Cecily.

"Good night, girls," he said. They heard the door close behind him.

Not thirty seconds later, the back door to the basement opened and Spencer Eton strolled in, followed by Drew Napolitano, Matt Graham, Richie Huber and Reese Highland.

"Evening, ladies," Richie said seductively.

"Pizza?" Reese said, grabbing a slice of pepperoni and taking a bite. "All right."

"I never thought I'd see the day when Coco De Clerq would be eating pizza in a basement," said Spencer.

"It's my Marie Antoinette moment," Coco said. "Only instead of cake and peasants, we have shag carpeting and Ping-Pong."

"We're not going to get you in trouble, are we?" Reese asked Haley.

"I hope not," she said. "Otherwise I won't be allowed out of the house for a month."

"And that wouldn't be good," Matt said suggestively.

Is he flirting with me? Haley wondered. *And why him instead of Reese?*

"So who's up for a little spin the bottle?" Richie asked, eyeing Whitney. "Seven minutes in heaven?"

"Ew," said Whitney. "I'm eating."

"We could watch a movie," said Haley.

"As entertaining as that sounds," said Spencer, picking up a few of the VHS tapes, "*Can't Buy Me Love* isn't really my speed. What do you say we all pile into Richie's car and go find a real party?"

"I'm in," Coco said without hesitating, tossing her half-eaten slice of pizza back onto her plate.

"Me too," Whitney added.

"I guess," said Matt.

"What about you, Haley?" Spencer asked. "You staying or going?"

Haley looked around the room, first at Coco, who was smiling defiantly with her arms folded across her chest, then at Cecily, who shrugged and said, "It's your call," and finally at Reese, who was now hungrily chomping on his second piece of pepperoni pizza.

"I think I should stay here," Haley said finally, "in case my dad checks up on us again."

"Then I'm staying with Haley," said Cecily.

"Well, I'm not letting all this good pizza go to waste," Reese said, plopping down in an easy chair. Coco looked annoyed.

"You guys go ahead," said Drew. "We'll hold the fort."

"Whatever, dude," Matt said, losing his patience. Haley noticed he kept stealing quick looks at her.

He has a crush on me, Haley suddenly realized.

She wondered if she wasn't making a mistake by staying home.

"Until the a.m.," Coco said, making her exit. She was followed by Whitney, who grabbed a slice of pepperoni pizza on her way out. Richie, right behind them, kept reaching out his hands as if to grab Whitney's butt and stopping himself each time he got within an inch of her flesh.

"Haley, thanks for the hospitality," said Spencer on his way out the door. "Drew, I'll see you tomorrow night."

Matt paused at the door and seemed about to say something, but then he looked at Reese, then back at Haley, and just walked out.

"What's tomorrow night?" Haley asked Drew.

"We're having SIGMA at my place," he said. "You're all invited."

"You're a brave soul," said Haley. "I don't know if I could handle half the school showing up on my lawn."

"It's a smaller crowd this time," said Drew, quickly adding with a smirk, "dress is casual. Very casual."

"Sounds like fun," said Cecily.

"I can't make it," said Reese. "I've got a makeup chem lab on Sunday. The downside of spending an extra week in Europe."

"So," Drew said, looking through the videotapes, "who's up for *Point Break*?"

"I am an F . . . B . . . I . . . agent," Reese said, mimicking Keanu Reeves's character in the classic surfers-as-bank-robbers heist flick.

"I'll pop the popcorn," said Haley, throwing a bag in the kitchenette's microwave as Drew and Cecily sat down on one of the couches.

"Awesome," said Reese. "I have to say, I'm digging the Miller basement. I might have to start spending more time over here."

Fine by me, Haley thought, sitting down beside him.

"By the way," Reese added, "I'm supposed to invite you and your family over for supper Sunday night. My folks think it's about time the Millers and Highlands all got together."

Any reservations Haley had about staying in instantly faded away.

● ● ●

It's a good thing Haley didn't pile into Richie's car with the others. Otherwise, she would have missed out on all that quality time with Reese.

So what should she do next?

The obvious choice would be to go to the MILLER-HIGHLAND DINNER on page 135. But if Drew's invitation to SIGMA sounds more appealing, since it could give Haley a chance to spend more time with Matt Graham, turn to page 120. If you're not ready to choose between Reese and Matt, send Haley back to school for PRINCIPAL CRUM'S LITANY on page 129.

So, the options are a schoolwide assembly, a hot boy at a party with parents, or a hot party with no parents and lots of boys. Which way do you think Haley should go?

THEFT IN THE CAFETERIA

To catch a thief,
you have to come up
with the bait.

The following Monday at school, Haley, in her new suede moccasin boots with jeans and a gray turtleneck, was standing in the cafeteria line looking at the options: chicken quesadillas, cheese pizza and Sloppy Joes.

The cafeteria food was technically pretty bad, but since Haley rarely, if ever, was without a packed lunch, she was savoring all the unhealthy possibilities before she settled on a meal.

"Whatcha havin', hon?" asked Rosie Dominello, the friendly, heavyset lunch lady in a black hairnet.

Rosie was a favorite among kids at school, unlike, say, the cashier, Fanny Pincus, who hated kids, hated the school, hated hawks and even hated the school colors, gold and blue.

"Pizza," Haley said as a big cheesy rectangle was carefully placed on the green plastic tray in front of her. Since she was still her mother's daughter, she also grabbed a carton of milk, an oatmeal cookie and an apple.

"That'll be six-fifty," Fanny Pincus demanded, without punching any buttons on the register. Haley noticed that Fanny had two plastic bank bags in front of her, one fuller than the other.

That's strange, Haley thought. *Why isn't she using the cash register? And why does she need an extra pouch for cash?*

It was as if Fanny read her mind. "Register's broken," she said. "Someone smashed it up last week."

Haley reluctantly handed over the money, glaring at Fanny.

At that moment, Sasha entered the cafeteria arm in arm with Luke.

They look awfully cozy, Haley thought, *especially since Sasha's supposed to be dating Johnny Lane.* Luke whispered something in Sasha's ear, then slipped through a door to the kitchen, leaving Sasha conspicuously waiting by the entrance.

She's been acting so strange lately, Haley thought, making her way to the condiments bar. *What happened to the Sasha Lewis we all knew and loved?*

Haley added some parmesan cheese to her pizza, then sprinkled red pepper flakes on top. But before she could find a place to sit and dig into her slice, the fire alarm sounded.

You've got to be kidding me, Haley thought, looking longingly at her hot lunch. *I don't care if the school is on fire, I'll eat my pizza while I watch it burn.* Haley defiantly carried the tray with her as she followed the herd of students heading toward the exit.

Out in the hallway, Garrett "the Troll" Noll and his friend Chopper, who were both from the Floods, popped out of an unmarked door. Chopper was shoving his wallet into his back pocket. *What are they up to?* Haley wondered as they eyed her lunch.

Chopper groaned. "Man, am I hungry."

"Hey, Red," Reese said, sneaking up on her. Seeing Reese, Chopper and the Troll dispersed.

"Thank goodness," said Haley, holding up her tray. "I need someone to help me with this."

Reese, thinking she was offering him the pizza, grabbed the slice and took a massive bite. "Awesome," he said. "How did you know I was starving?"

"Um," Haley said tentatively, "actually . . ."

"That reminds me, you are coming to our house for dinner this Sunday, aren't you?" Reese asked. "My mom wanted me to remind you."

Like I could ever forget, Haley thought. She'd been looking forward to the Miller-Highland joint family dinner ever since her mother had told her about the invitation.

"There you are, Reese," Coco said, slinking up behind him and wrapping her arms around his waist.

"Oooh, pizza," Whitney said. Haley watched helplessly as Whitney leaned in and took a bite from the slice in Reese's hands.

"Dude, Klein, what are you doing? That's Haley's lunch," Reese said as Whitney snatched another bite.

"That's disgusting," said Coco.

Reese gave Haley back a gnarled piece of crust and not much else. "Sorry," he said.

"Highland, is there anything you won't eat?" Spencer Eton asked, approaching the group. "Ladies, you're all looking luscious today, as usual."

"Hey, Spence," Whitney said, grabbing Haley's only napkin to dab the corners of her mouth.

"I trust I'll see you all at SIGMA this week," said Spencer. "It's at Drew Napolitano's this time." He winked at Haley.

"I thought you were keeping this one small," said Coco. "No . . . undesirables."

"Smallish," said Spencer. He looked at Haley again and said, "You know how to dress."

"Hi, guys," Cecily Watson said, walking up with a hefty sack of books. "So did you hear what happened?"

"Let me guess. The cafeteria just got robbed again," Coco said matter-of-factly.

"Yep," said Cecily. "Third time this month."

Whitney suddenly spotted the oatmeal cookie on Haley's tray.

"You're kidding," said Haley, setting down the tray and clutching her milk, apple and dessert protectively.

"Who would do something like that?" Reese asked.

"I don't know. Some people just see something they want and take it," Haley said, looking directly at Whitney.

"This is what we get for going to public school," Coco said, turning to face Haley, "and mixing with the riffraff."

"The cops are here," Reese said. He pointed to the two squad cars that had just pulled into the parking lot.

"Wow, this is, like, serious," Whitney said.

"Who do you think did it?" Reese asked.

Coco, still facing Haley, said, "Well, we know at least one person who was in the cafeteria at the time of the alarm."

Haley rolled her eyes. "Very funny."

She looked around at the Troll and Chopper, who were now harassing a freshman not far from where Haley stood. Sasha and Luke came out of the gym and immediately split up, with Sasha heading to meet Johnny on the lawn, and Luke carrying a backpack to his beat-up van in the parking lot. Fanny Pincus, who was leaning on a nearby silver sedan and smoking a cigarette, looked at Luke, shook her head and stamped out the butt.

"I don't know for sure," said Haley, "but I've got a pretty good idea."

• • •

Breaking into the cafeteria while school's in session? Now, that's a bold thief. So whodunnit? Was it those troublemakers from the Floods, the Troll and Chopper? What about Fanny, the loveless lunchroom attendant? Or did Luke and Sasha mastermind the heist together?

To find out more about the latest crime and punishment saga at Hillsdale High, turn to PRINCIPAL CRUM'S LITANY (page 129). To leave the detective work to the real detectives, go to the MILLER-HIGHLAND DINNER on page 135. Alternatively, send Haley to SIGMA (page 120), and find out what it means to dress, or should we say undress, for success.

ALONE WITH LUKE

If you're going to dance with the devil, better make sure you're in a crowded ballroom.

As Luke led Haley down the hall to Sasha's spare room, she felt the cell phone in her bag vibrate.

"I should probably get that," she said, reaching for her purse.

"Forget it," Luke said, taking the phone and the bag out of her hands. "Come here." He wrapped his arms around her waist. Before Haley knew what was happening, Luke was kissing her and maneuvering her onto the bed.

"Wait," Haley said, but each time Luke kissed her she forgot a little more of what she was going to say.

Haley barely noticed when he slid his hand down the waistband of her jeans. He was still kissing her when her jeans came off. At some point her bag vibrated again, but Luke just shoved it under the bed as he peeled off her sweater.

"I promise," he whispered. "We won't do anything you don't want to do." Then he switched on the stereo and turned up the volume on an old U2 song while taking off his own sweaty T-shirt.

Maybe it was the loud music. Maybe it was Luke's kisses. Maybe it was wanting so badly to forget everything that seemed to be going wrong in Hillsdale.

But for whatever reason, Haley didn't hear the pounding on the front door of the Lewis condo fifteen minutes later. She didn't hear the voices in the living room. And she definitely didn't hear the heavy footsteps coming down the hall.

She did, however, hear her father's voice just before he burst into the room. "Haley, are you in there?"

Unfortunately, there wasn't sufficient time to get dressed.

● ● ●

Uh-oh. What were you thinking? Haley isn't even dating Luke. She barely knows him! And yet you left her alone with that shady character?

Not only did Haley's dad just catch her hooking up with a juvenile delinquent, but take a guess why he was so frantic to find her.

When Haley didn't show up at the therapist's office, Mitchell Miller decided to walk home on his own, by way of the playground. While swinging on the jungle gym, he fell and broke his arm.

Of course, after Perry discovered Sasha living on her own, without parental supervision, he called Social Services, and Sasha was put in foster care until her mother flew to the United States. For revenge, Sasha ruined Haley's reputation by telling everyone at school that Haley had done "everything but" with a guy she hardly knew.

And Haley's father? After having the image of his sweet little girl, half naked and in the arms of Luke Lawson, burned into his brain, he never looked at her quite the same way.

Hang your head and go back to page 1.

Welcome to the Twilight Zone, also known as the Rick Von Time Trap.

"This place is even weirder than I imagined," Haley said, adjusting her new tweed skirt as she and Sebastian arrived in front of Mr. Von's Craftsman-style bungalow in the Heights.

Steel sculptures sprouted up from Mr. Von's unkempt lawn, and a pair of paint-chipped Adirondack chairs sat on the front porch, sharing space with an antique bicycle, a Victorian metal birdcage and a rooster weathervane that squeaked in the late-autumn breeze.

Haley had an uneasy feeling. "Remind me why we need Mr. Von's help again," she said, looking at

Sebastian, hoping he'd say they should just turn around and forget the whole thing.

"Don't worry. It is only Mr. Von," he said, taking her hand.

Exactly, Haley thought, following Sebastian up the steps.

Inside, an old Mama Cass record warbled through the cluttered rooms. They followed the sound of her overly sunny voice until they reached a dimly lit den, where Mr. Von was sitting on the floor, eyes closed, next to an old record player with a green and red parrot perched on his shoulder.

Freaky, Haley thought, feeling like she'd just slipped into another dimension.

There was a sudden rustle behind her. She jumped. Mr. Von reached for the turntable and scratched the record, causing the parrot to begin shrieking violently. Haley spun around to find two figures wearing what looked like white hazmat suits—rubber jumpers with booties, gloves and plastic masks where there should have been faces—sitting on the couch. She screamed. The white figures got up off the sofa, with some difficulty, and walked toward her. Haley cowered behind Sebastian, until one of them lifted up the face mask to reveal . . . Dave Metzger's goofy grin.

"Hi, Haley, Sebastian," Dave said, beaming. Haley realized that the other figure must be Hannah, and just as she was starting to relax, something bolted out of the shadows from the opposite corner of the room. Haley screamed again as Annie Armstrong latched on to her and Sebastian. "I thought you'd never get here," Annie whispered. Her face was sheet white.

"Haley, Sebastian, welcome," Mr. Von said in his soothing voice. He got up from the floor and walked toward them favoring his right leg, with the bird still on his shoulder. "This is Constantine," he said, swooping down so that the bird was at eye level with Haley. "Say hello, Constantine."

"Hello, Constantine," the bird squawked.

It was at that moment that Haley had a startling revelation. The explanation for Mr. Von's slight limp? The parrot? The patch he occasionally wore to correct his lazy eye? Hillsdale's art teacher was a pirate.

Just then Mrs. Metzger burst through a set of swinging double doors. "Honestly, Rick, I have no idea how you live this way. I couldn't find anything in that kitchen except canned beans, ginger beer and a few jugs of rum." She stopped short when she saw Haley and Sebastian. "Oh. Hello," she said.

Yo ho ho and a bottle of rum, Haley thought suspiciously, looking at Mr. Von.

"Now that we're all here, shall we retire to the studio?" he asked.

"Fine by me," Annie said, anxious to get what they'd come for and get the heck out of there.

Mr. Von held out his arm for Mrs. Metzger, which she gladly accepted. "You know, you could do with a little help around the house," she said, patting his hand.

"Are you offering?" he asked.

"Oh my," said Mrs. Metzger, blushing.

As they walked through the densely wooded property to an old shed that served as Mr. Von's painting and sculpture studio, Haley whispered to Sebastian and Annie, "How does an art teacher afford three acres in the Heights?"

"Maybe he's behind all the recent thefts at school," Annie suggested.

"You girls," Sebastian chuckled. "Do you really think a man who has studied with the Shaolin monks would steal from a high school cafeteria register?"

"It could happen," said Annie.

"So what's with the marshmallow twins?" Haley asked Annie, motioning toward Hannah and Dave, who were awkwardly trying to negotiate the footpath in their bulky white suits.

"Mrs. Metzger wouldn't let them in the house till Mr. Von dug out his old radiation suits. Too much dust. Did you know Acid Rick once worked at a nuclear power plant?"

"Nothing would surprise me about that guy," Haley said.

When they reached the studio, Mr. Von entered ahead of them and flipped on the lights.

It was, Haley had to admit, sort of cool. There was an easel set up in one corner. A large pine table was cluttered with sketchpads, charcoal pencils, half-squeezed tubes of paint and strange little figurines sculpted out of modeling clay. And near the door was a wood-burning stove, next to several big sheets of metal, a sledgehammer and a fire iron.

While the others wandered around, exploring the space, Mr. Von opened up a dusty old storage chest marked *Seville*. "So here is the buried treasure," Haley said, kneeling down beside him. She pulled out an old matador's embroidered jacket and short pants as Sebastian and Annie sifted through stacks of old newspapers, photographs, and Spanish pesos.

"Look at all this stuff," Haley marveled, holding up a grainy black-and-white photo of an old man selling fruits and vegetables.

Sebastian smiled. "This is very near my house. Someday, you will come and visit me in Spain, and I will take you to this market," he said.

"Why don't we start with a trip to the movies," Haley said, putting on the brakes.

"How is Sunday?" Sebastian said, kissing her hand.

"Can't," Haley said, remembering that her family was supposed to have dinner next door with the Highlands that night. In fact, she was actually sort of looking forward to hanging out with Reese.

"But I cannot wait for the moment when we are finally alone together," Sebastian whispered in her ear.

Annie rolled her eyes.

"I think Dave and Annie should come too," Haley said. Sebastian frowned.

"Gee," said Annie, "I'd love to go on a double date with you guys and all, but seeing as how my boyfriend appears to be surgically attached to Hannah Moss these days, I think I'll have to decline."

They all turned to look at the marshmallow twins, who had finally reached the door to the studio. Dave was trying to help Hannah up the steps, but her boot got wedged in the door jamb.

As he knelt down to pry it out, Haley whispered in Sebastian's ear, "Please ask Dave to come with us. Ever since Hannah joined the group, Dave and Annie have hardly seen each other. I'm worried about them."

"As you wish," Sebastian said.

Haley turned to Annie. "Don't worry, Annie," she said, reassuring her friend. "He'll come to his senses eventually."

But as Hannah steadied herself, leaning on Dave's shoulder, even Haley wondered just what exactly was going on.

● ● ●

What do you think? Are Hannah Moss and Dave now a couple? Or is Dave just temporarily distracted? Will he ever be hopelessly devoted to Annie again, and what can Haley do to help?

Find out by sending Haley on a DOUBLE DATE on page 139. Or look into those mysterious thefts at school Annie mentioned in PRINCIPAL CRUM'S LITANY (page 129). Alternatively, you can have Haley hang out with Reese at the MILLER-HIGHLAND DINNER on page 135.

If you think thirty minutes down the rabbit hole at

Mr. Von's was strange, wait until Haley's in a dark theater with Sebastian, Annie and Dave. Just remember, if Haley spends all her time trying to fix someone else's relationship, she might blow her chance at having one of her own.

THE MILLER HOUSEHOLD

Home is where the
heartthrob is.

"Look, Mitchell, I got the purple shield," Haley said. She was sitting on the floor in the basement, playing video games with her baby brother.

"Excellent. Princess Shimmer," Mitchell said in his robot voice as an octopus attacked his player on the simulated ocean screen. "Oh no. I am fish food," he said as his life force expired.

A little quality time together was the least she could do after almost landing Mitchell in the hospital that afternoon. *It's a good thing your life force* didn't *expire,* she thought, looking at Mitchell.

Haley had been only a few minutes late to pick

him up from his therapy session. But, as usual, Mitchell had gotten antsy.

Luckily, Haley had found him climbing on the jungle gym at a nearby playground. She shuddered to think what might have happened if she hadn't been there to get him down.

"You having fun, Mitch?" she asked as she used the controls to dive away from the octopus. Mitchell watched closely, advising Haley on where she could pick up extra points.

"That is. The sea eel," he said. "You must ask. For directions."

"Knock, knock," Reese said, peeking his head through the door to the basement.

Haley looked up just as her character came before the sea eel. "Hey, Reese!"

"Noooo!" Mitchell said, grabbing Haley's paddles. "You only have. Fifteen seconds. Before the sea eel. Destroys you." But it was too late. The eel electrocuted Princess Shimmer. "Now we will. Never know. The way to. Fathom's Canyon."

A hammerhead shark swam across the screen waving a red pennant flag that said "Game Over."

"The sea eel get you again, buddy?" Reese asked, sitting down and taking the controls. "Watch and learn, Mitchell. Watch and learn."

The three of them cozied up on the sofa as Reese reset the video game and started playing.

"Hey, nice moves," Haley said as Reese zapped a school of blowfish.

"Watch this," Reese said, launching into a flying underwater ninja kick. He swam straight down to the ocean floor, opened a pirate's treasure chest and picked up a golden key. "That's a little shortcut I discovered last year." Within seconds, Reese was back in front of the sea eel, a feat that had taken Haley more than twenty-five minutes to accomplish.

Haley looked over and saw that Mitchell was actually *smiling* for once.

"Reese. You are. A formidable player," Mitchell said.

"Just glad I could help," said Reese, ruffling Mitchell's hair and handing over the controls.

"Hey, thanks," Haley whispered.

"No problem," he said. "He's a good kid."

"So is that why you came over? To play video games with my brother?"

"Actually . . ." Reese hesitated, smiling at her.

Haley's heart was pounding. *Maybe he wants to ask me out?* she wondered. *Maybe he wants to make out with me. Maybe he wants to ask me out so he can make out with me.*

"My parents have been wanting to do a big Miller-Highland get-together ever since your family moved into the neighborhood. I'm here to find out if you're free Sunday night."

"That's so . . . thoughtful," Haley said. "And neighborly." She, of course, had been hoping for a different sort of invitation. "Is that the only reason you stopped by?"

"Well. There is something I've been wanting to talk to you about," Reese added. "Something important."

"Really?" Haley leaned toward him, hanging on those last two words.

"It's about . . ." Reese paused.

"Yes?" Haley asked, tortured by the anticipation.

"Sasha," Reese said finally.

"Oh." Haley's heart sank. "You're worried about her, aren't you?"

"Haven't you noticed how much school she's missed lately?"

"Sure," said Haley. "I've tried checking up on her, but she doesn't seem to want my help."

"There must be something we can do," said Reese.

"Like what?" Haley asked. She couldn't believe her luck. Here she finally had Reese's attention, and all he wanted to do was talk about another girl. Still, deep down, she knew Reese was right. Sasha did need their help.

First we take care of Sasha, then who knows? At least, that's what Haley kept telling herself.

• • •

If you think Haley and Reese should consult their parents on what to do next, turn to the MILLER-HIGHLAND DINNER on page 135. If you think that will take too long and want Haley to INVESTIGATE SASHA on her own instead, turn to page 172.

The sooner Haley solves the Sasha mystery, the sooner she and Reese can be together. Just make sure that in rushing to find answers, Haley doesn't create new problems for herself and her friends.

PLEASE, PLEASE, PLEASE

Sometimes a girl should be too proud to beg.

"Just when were you planning to tell us about this coed trip to California? On your way to the airport?" Joan said once they were in the kitchen.

"I was going to tell you," said Haley. "I was just waiting for the right moment."

"You were going to *tell* me? About a weekend trip to San Francisco with boys I only met today? What happened to *asking* your parents for permission?"

Haley said bitterly, "Did you and Dad *ask* me if I wanted to move to New Jersey?" She could tell by the look on her mother's face that she'd gone too far.

"Haley, I think it's time you asked your friends to leave."

"But they just got here!"

"And while you're at it," Joan added, "you can give them back that plane ticket to California. Because you're grounded. I don't like your attitude."

Haley's heart sank. She *couldn't* miss out on this trip to San Francisco, she just couldn't. "Mom, please, please, please, don't do this," she begged. "I'm sorry. I'll do anything you want me to. Just please let me go."

"You heard me, Haley," Joan said sternly. "Maybe if you had come to me first and been honest . . ."

"I'm being honest now."

"It's too late."

"But, Mom—"

"Haley, you heard me."

Haley finally gave up and moped into the living room to deliver the bad news: Not only would she not be going to California, but she was likely grounded through the holidays.

● ● ●

Too bad. For the next few weeks, Haley's social life is going to revolve around video games with Mitchell. And who wants to watch her cry into her pillow every night?

Go back to page 1.

Now matter how hard we try not to, sometimes we outgrow our old friends.

"Okay, Kath," Joan said with the kitchen phone pressed to her ear. "I'm glad the girls are going to see each other too. It has been a long four months. So we'll talk later this week? Okay. Bye now."

Haley could tell by the look on her mom's face that she'd won: Her parents were going to let her go to California. She was, in a word, ecstatic. "I can go? Really?" she said, nearly tackling her mother with a hug.

"All right, all right," Joan said, taking a step back. "I know you were disappointed we said no to the hotel room with your friends. But I'd just feel better about you staying at Gretchen's. It's not that we don't trust you, Haley. We just don't want you in any compromising situations."

Haley suddenly sensed an awkward B and B talk coming. As in the birds and the bees. "Um, I should probably check on my friends," she said, trying to look casual.

"Devon seems like a nice boy. Are you two getting . . . close? Because you know you can always talk to me," Joan said, taking a large saucepan out of a cupboard. "About anything," she added, emphasis on the word *anything*.

"Ew, Mom. That's why we have health class at school." At that moment, Haley's cell phone rang. "Once again, saved by the cell."

"Hi, Haley." The voice on the other end of the line was sugary sweet.

"Who is this?" Haley asked.

"It's Coco De Clerq."

"Seriously, Irene, you pulled the same lame joke on me last week. Can't you come up with some new material?"

"Irene who?" Coco asked. "Wait, do you mean that weird chick from school? Do you really hang out with her? Because you're, like, totally pretty. You could be popular and have any guy you wanted."

"Whatever," Haley said, pretending not to care. But it was a tempting scenario. *Really? Any guy I wanted?* she wondered.

"I know of at least five who are totally crushing on you," Coco said.

"Oh, yeah, right. Like who?" said Haley.

"Well, Matt Graham for one. And Drew Napolitano."

"I thought he liked Whitney?"

"That was last year," Coco said. "Why, do you like him?"

"No, he's . . . not my type."

"See, Whitney," Coco said. "I told you she didn't like Drew."

Haley gasped. This whole time, Whitney Klein had also been on the line, listening in.

"What do you mean he's not your type?" Whitney asked. "Do you think there's something wrong with him?"

"Klein, enough," said Coco. "If you like Drew so much, go out with him yourself."

"Is that why you called me up?" Haley asked suspiciously. "To find out if I liked Drew Napolitano?"

"Actually, Haley . . ." Coco paused. "I don't know if you've heard yet, but my little sweet sixteen party is in a couple of weeks."

"Really? I hadn't heard," Haley lied. In fact, everyone at Hillsdale knew all about the party the De Clerqs were planning for Coco's sixteenth birthday. Even "I hate Coco De Clerq and everything she stands for" Irene was secretly hoping to snag an invite. That was just so that she could spend the whole night sitting in the corner, making fun of all the Cocobots.

"We're working on her guest list," said Whitney.

"We want to know if you're sweet sixteen material," said Coco.

"So what is this, like an audition?" Haley asked. She wondered if Coco could possibly be serious. Or if she had any idea how transparent she was.

"What are you up to this weekend?" Coco asked.

"I'm supposed to fly out to California."

"Really?" said Coco. "Wicked. Who are you going with?"

"Some . . . friends." For some reason, Haley couldn't bring herself to name Irene, Shaun and Devon.

"Let me guess. Irene Chen?" Haley didn't answer. "I have a better idea," said Coco. "Meet me at Drip. We'll have coffee and plan my party—"

"But Coco, you said it was going to be just you and me this time," Whitney interrupted. "But you already invited Cecily Watson to sleep over last weekend," Whitney whined.

"Shut up, Whitney."

"Wait—Cecily?" Haley asked curiously. "What happened to Sasha Lewis? I thought the three of you shared a brain."

"Not anymore," muttered Whitney. "Maybe that's why I'm failing math."

"Sasha's been getting on our last nerve lately," Coco explained. "Ever since her dad blew all their money in Atlantic City and she started dating that skeeze, Johnny Lane. She's gone total *Bad Seed*."

"We think Sasha is behind all those thefts at school," said Whitney.

"Really?" Haley asked. "What makes you say that?"

"Um, hello? A girl's got to eat," said Whitney.

"Ugh, thank God Johnny's band isn't playing your sweet sixteen. Rubber Dynamite is way cooler. Do you realize how awesome your party is going to be?"

"I know, right?" said Coco. "So what do you say, Haley? California with freaks? Or coffee with Coco?"

"You should feel really special, Haley," Whitney said. "She doesn't extend these sorts of invitations to just anyone, you know."

● ● ●

Unfortunately, Haley can't be in two places at once. If she goes to San Francisco, she'll miss out on all that happens in Hillsdale while she's away, and she can say goodbye to that invitation to Coco's sweet sixteen. But if she stays in Hillsdale, Irene, Shaun and Devon will continue on their adventure without Haley. So what should she do?

To have her HEAD TO CALIFORNIA, turn to page 143. If you think she should take Coco up on her offer, go to COFFEE WITH COCO on page 231. Otherwise, have Haley INVESTIGATE SASHA Lewis on page 172.

So what will it be, East or West? In either direction, the cast of characters in Haley's world is, once again, about to change.

In strip poker, you hope for a flush but often end up blushing.

"**S**exy," Whitney complimented Haley, who was strutting toward Coco in high heels, a black miniskirt and the low-cut purple top her mom had just bought for her at the mall.

"Yeah, it was about time you updated your wardrobe, Miller," Coco said, looking at herself in her compact mirror. "Although I'm surprised your parents let you out of the house dressed like that."

Haley smiled. "Are you kidding? I had three layers of wool on over this when I walked out the door."

"Clothes are like oranges," said Whitney, applying

another coat of gloss to her lips. "You just keep peeling until you get to the juicy parts."

"For once, Whitney, your metaphor actually works. Haley, maybe you should've waited to shed some of those layers," Coco said, exchanging a knowing glance with Whitney.

"What do you mean?" Haley asked.

"You'll see," Whitney teased, puckering her lips and kissing the air.

"It can get a little chilly at Drew's," said Coco.

It was at that moment that Haley noticed the many, many layers Coco and Whitney were wearing. Coco had on a double-ply cashmere sweater over a tank top, with a big belt slung around her waist. Her denim miniskirt was layered over black leggings, and for accessories, she wore big hoop earrings, a fedora and low-heeled pumps.

Whitney, too, seemed to have piled on half her closet. She wore a headband, a ribbon necklace, a rabbit-fur vest over a white T-shirt, tight jeans, leg warmers and ballet flats.

Coco rang the Napolitanos' doorbell impatiently.

"SIGMA hotties in the house," Drew said when he opened the door.

"Drew," Coco greeted him breezily. Whitney presented her cheek to Drew, as usual. But instead of kissing her, Drew ignored her and smiled flirtatiously in Haley's direction.

"Haley, right? So glad you could make it," he said.

Whitney pretended not to notice, but Haley

could tell she was troubled by his newfound admiration for the new girl. Drew had, after all, always liked Whitney. Everyone knew that. And Whitney, for her part, tolerated his crush, without exactly encouraging him or rebuffing his advances. This was the way things had always been. That was, until now.

He's cute enough, Haley thought, flattered to be getting attention from one of the most popular boys in the sophomore class, *but not my type.*

Haley let Drew kiss her on the cheek as she walked through the door, though she suddenly had the sensation that Drew was looking over her shoulder at someone else.

Haley turned around to see Cecily Watson strutting up the driveway as if it were a red carpet or a catwalk. Cecily was wearing a pair of black leather pants, spiky high heels and a white mohair sweater that made her dark, smooth skin glow. Her perfect complexion had little makeup on it, other than her trademark lip gloss and a faint coat of mascara.

Cecily flashed her captivating smile at Drew as she glided up the steps. "Thanks for the invite," she said, winking at him.

"I didn't think you were coming," Drew said, unable to take his eyes off her.

"I finished my physics homework early, so I figured, why not? Hi, Haley. Love your top."

"Thanks," said Haley.

It was hard not to like Cecily. Sure, she was tall, gorgeous, had incredible style, and was already a cocaptain of the varsity cheerleading squad even though she was only a sophomore. But Cecily was also a good student, and went out of her way to be nice to everyone, absolutely everyone, at school, and not in a fake way. In fact, Haley had yet to find a flaw.

"Shall we?" Drew said, taking Cecily and Haley on either arm and leading them into the party.

In the Napolitanos' hunter green dining room, an intense game of poker was well underway between Spencer and two of his private school friends, Matt and Toby. However, it wasn't so intense that they didn't look up when the girls walked in.

"Hey," said Matt. He was looking, in particular, at Haley.

"So, Coco, have you thought any more about having the Hedon play at your birthday next month?" Toby asked.

Toby was the drummer in the local rock band, the Hedon, and he was just as comfortable hanging out in the Floods as he was in the parlors of Hillsdale's finest McMansions.

"Actually, Toby, I think I'm going in a different direction," Coco said.

"Don't tell me you've hired Rubber Dynamite?" Toby said, putting down his cards. "They're all keyboards and synthesizers. That's not real music. It's sound engineering."

"Well, I happen to like the way they sound," Coco said. "Besides, there's no way Johnny Lane and Luke Lawson are setting foot inside my party."

"De Clerq's right, man," Matt said. "Lawson is law-*less*. I don't know why you hang with him. He's six months away from knocking over convenience stores."

"Hey, I never said I liked the dude," Toby added. "But he's our lead guitarist. I can't kick him out of the band without Johnny backing me up."

"All I know is, there were no thefts at Hillsdale High until Luke showed up," said Spencer.

"Dude, you are so right!" said Drew.

"Hey, lady luck," Spencer said to Coco. "Get over here and work your magic so I can annihilate Matt and Toby."

"Gosh, Spencer, with an invitation like that, how could I resist?" Coco said, her voice dripping with sarcasm.

"It's sort of sad with only us this time," Whitney said. "Half the fun of SIGMA is watching all those pathetic losers get turned away."

"We had to downsize," Spencer said, glancing at his cards. "I can't afford to get busted twice in one semester. Coco, you're losing your touch. I fold."

"Now, Spencer, you know you've never experienced my touch," Coco said playfully.

"Right. One De Clerq sister's enough for any man," Toby said under his breath.

Haley assumed he was referring to Coco's sister, Alison, who had a habit of flirting with Coco's guy friends.

Coco's face turned bright red. Haley couldn't tell if she was embarrassed or infuriated. "Clearly, hanging out in the Floods has been good for you, Toby. Anyone need a drink? I'm suddenly very thirsty," Coco said with a clenched jaw. Without waiting for a reply, she headed toward the kitchen with Whitney practically stepping on her heels.

"Dude, you're killing me," Spencer said.

"Sorry, man," said Toby. "I speak the truth."

"Call," said Matt, laying down a full house, jacks high. Toby revealed four tens, sweeping the pot.

"Why don't we we step it up a notch now that the girls are here?" Spencer asked casually.

"Time's a-wasting," said Drew, staring at Cecily.

"Haley, would you mind fetching Coco and Whitney?" Spencer asked.

Haley didn't enjoy being talked to like a child, but she did want to check on Coco, so she obediently went off in search of the kitchen and her friends.

"You've really got to stop staring at Drew and Cecily like that or everyone's going to know you're just jealous," Coco said to Whitney just as Haley walked in.

So much for being worried about Coco, Haley thought.

"I can't help it," Whitney said. "Why doesn't he like me anymore?"

"Um, maybe because you've been blowing him off for, like, the past seven years?"

"Why do guys always seem so much cooler when

they like someone else?" Haley offered, trying to neutralize the conversation.

"Trust me, Whitney," said Coco, "if you really want Drew, the only way to get his attention is by not trying to get his attention."

"That doesn't make any sense," Whitney said. "Shouldn't I just tell him I like him? And then we can date, get married, have babies and live happily ever after?"

"Why do I bother?" Coco said, opening the door to the Napolitanos' climate-controlled wine closet. "Just leave it to me," she said, grabbing a bottle of merlot. "When I'm through with Drew, he won't even remember Cecily Watson's name."

Haley frowned, feeling a pang of sympathy for Cecily. *Aren't we all supposed to be friends?* she wondered.

"Wow, this bottle is older than I am," Whitney said, picking up a vintage Château Latour.

"This one is pretty ancient too," Haley said, blowing a cloud of dust off another bottle. "Grand Cru Classé."

"Not those," Coco said. "Drew's parents will know they're missing. Look for California reds with recent years on the labels." She grabbed two bottles of champagne out of the minifridge.

When they returned to the poker table, Cecily was sitting next to Drew, and Matt was on his left.

"Cecily," Coco said, "you and Drew switch places so that we're boy-girl, boy-girl." They obliged, which opened up a seat next to Drew for Whitney, just as

Coco had planned. Haley took her place between Matt and Spencer. And Coco sat down between Spencer and Toby.

"Here's the drill," said Spencer. "We bet with clothes."

Haley's face went white. Suddenly she understood why Coco and Whitney were wearing three outfits at once.

"You don't want to put a piece into the pot," Spencer continued, "you have to drink. A lot," he said, pouring six paper cups full of champagne. "As in, finish what's in this cup."

"Haley, why don't you ante up first," Coco said, watching Drew to see how he would react.

Haley wondered if this was part of the plan: Distract Drew from Cecily by getting him to focus on naked Haley instead. *Why do I get stuck being bait?* she wondered.

Everyone, Drew included, was now staring at Haley, trying to guess which piece of her outfit would be the first to come off, and wondering if she'd chicken out and choose to drink instead. Only Matt's gaze was sympathetic.

"Come on, Haley," Coco said provocatively. "What are you waiting for? Take it off."

● ● ●

To have Haley ante up with something she's wearing, turn to TAKE IT OFF (page 149). To have her drink instead, send her to DRINK AT SIGMA (page 155). If you think this crowd is too fast for Haley, have her GO HOME for a little downtime with her family on page 237.

There's no telling what can happen when booze mixes with bare skin, so if you choose to have Haley stay, be prepared for her to accept the consequences.

PRINCIPAL CRUM'S LITANY

To rebel or not to rebel,
that is the question.

On Monday morning, Principal Crum called a schoolwide assembly to talk about the recent string of thefts at Hillsdale High.

"There's some space up top," Ms. Lipsky, Haley's homeroom teacher, said, pointing to an opening in the nosebleed section. There were six open seats between the misfits and the waistoids. Haley's teacher shrugged almost apologetically before taking her seat with the other instructors.

Walking up the steps, Haley noticed a few of the Floods kids from her bus route. There was Garrett "the Troll" Noll, flanked by Dale and Chopper. Johnny Lane was stretched out and snoozing in his seat.

That's odd, Sasha's not with him, Haley thought. Rarely in the past few weeks had she seen the two of them apart.

She kept walking past Darla, the supersized senior who ate freshman boys for breakfast, lunch, dinner and the occasional snack in between. And skinny, bespectacled Dale, who sat next to her in some of her classes.

There's one good thing about the nosebleeds, Haley thought as she sat down next to Dale. *You can see everyone, but they can't necessarily see you.*

Haley spotted Sebastian sitting in a section full of junior girls. He was flirting shamelessly. *Figures,* she thought.

Dave Metzger was sitting between Annie Armstrong and a diminutive girl named Hannah Moss. They both seemed to be vying for his attention. Haley made a mental note to find out what was going on with Annie and Dave.

Coco, Whitney and Cecily Watson were sitting near the front, whispering and giggling. *Sasha's not with Coco and Whitney either,* Haley realized. *And it looks as if they've already found her replacement.*

That made the invitation Haley had received that morning all the more interesting. Out of the blue, Cecily had stopped by Haley's locker and invited her to a sleepover that weekend. *I wonder if that means Coco and Whitney will be there?* Haley thought, watching Cecily gossip with the popular girls.

Principal Crum approached the podium. The microphone hummed and sent feedback through the speakers, several of which were mounted right near Haley's head. She rubbed her ears, fearing she might be temporarily deaf.

"Students," Principal Crum began, "when miniskirt hemlines climbed dangerously high last year, what did we do?" He paused for effect. "We instituted a temporary dress code."

"And luckily no one followed it," Chopper said. Haley looked over and noticed he was wearing a shiny new gold watch.

"When vandalism came to Hillsdale earlier this semester," Principal Crum continued, "what did we do?" He paused again, glancing around at various students. "We smote it out."

"Shaun turned himself in?" Chopper yelled, cupping his hands around his mouth.

"Dang it, students, this is no laughing matter," Principal Crum said, pounding his fist on the podium. "As of this morning, we are back on turquoise alert. And I'm even thinking of raising it to aubergine.

"In the past month, twelve hundred and fifty dollars has been stolen from this campus, out of your lockers, the teachers' lounge, the school cafeteria. Canned goods were even taken from the holiday food drive pantry. Someone out there took strained peaches out of a poor, sick baby's mouth, and I can't have that.

"Now, the punishment that fits this crime is not going to be a couple of Saturday detentions. We've called in the law." Principal Crum motioned to the side of the gym, where two cops were standing.

"Officer Stack, Officer Larchmont, do you have something to say to our students?" Principal Crum urged.

The two policemen walked over to the podium, and one of them leaned into the microphone and said, "Good morning. Please, if you could, keep a tight rein on your belongings over the next few days. Watch out for any suspicious activity. Report anything out of the ordinary, anything at all, to your homeroom teachers. And rest assured, we won't rest until we catch the person or persons responsible. Thank you. Go, Hawks."

Principal Crum resumed his stance behind the mike. "Thank you, Officer Larchmont, particularly for your show of Hawks spirit. Now, students, I want you to think about what these two gentlemen said on your way back to class. Dismissed."

As the assembly began to disperse, Haley noticed that the Troll was carrying what looked to be a brand-new skateboard.

They've certainly become high rollers, she thought, making her way to the bottom of the steps, where Reese was waiting for her.

"Just the girl I was looking for," he said with a heart-stopping smile.

Haley wondered if this was finally going to be the moment when Reese Highland asked her out. She straightened her skirt and smoothed out her hair, wanting to look perfect in case this was it.

"What can I do for you?" she asked casually.

"You look great," he said. "Love the haircut."

Her stomach was in knots. The anticipation was almost unbearable. Reese shifted his stance and put his hands in his pockets. "Are you free Sunday night?" he asked.

"I think so," Haley said, trying not to seem too eager. "Why?"

"Well, my mom wanted me to invite you and your family over to our house for dinner," Reese explained.

"Oh," Haley said. *So that's what this is about?* She tried to hide her disappointment.

"Hey, you seen Sasha lately?" Reese asked.

"No, actually," said Haley, happy for the distraction. "She's been missing a lot of school lately."

"It's so weird," he said. "Six months ago, I never would've guessed I would be worried about Sasha Lewis."

"You're starting to think maybe Sasha had something to do with the thefts."

"You too?" he asked.

Haley shrugged. "I don't realy know what to think," she said. "But maybe there's something we can do to help."

"Like what?" said Reese.

"I don't know. But something tells me we better think fast."

• • •

To send Haley to INVESTIGATE SASHA on her own, turn to page 172. If you think Haley and Reese should consider asking their parents for help figuring out the Sasha situation, go to the MILLER-HIGHLAND DINNER (page 135). Alternatively, send Haley to a sleepover at CECILY WATSON'S HOUSE on page 159, or have her find out what's going on with Annie and Dave at the ICE CREAM PARLOR (page 178).

Will Haley end up in Reese's arms? Will Annie lose Dave forever? Will Sasha self-destruct? And will the popular girls embrace Haley as one of their own? It all depends on how you choose here.

MILLER-HIGHLAND DINNER

You can live inches away from someone and still not know what they're really like.

"Reese, why don't you show Haley our Europe pictures while I check on the quiche?" Barbara Highland, a petite brunette, said.

"Everything smells delicious, Barbara. What can I do to help?" Joan Miller asked, following her into the kitchen.

"So, Perry," Oliver Highland, Reese's silver-haired father, said, pulling up a chair next to his guest. "You're a tree man. What do you make of this elm disease that's threatening the neighborhood?"

Haley knew from experience that her father

could talk elm disease all night. However, as long as she had a cozy seat on the sofa next to Reese, she didn't care how long they stayed.

Haley was thrilled to finally be inside the Highlands' living room. Granted, it was a family dinner that got her there, but she was optimistic. *Maybe this will become a regular thing,* she thought, watching Mitchell actually behaving himself for once, and quietly playing on the floor with the "toys" he'd brought over from next door: a wooden coat hanger, a green plastic soap dish and a half dozen rubber bands.

Haley was temporarily pulled from the happy little scene by a faint vibration on her hip. She pulled out her cell phone to look at the screen and saw that Cecily Watson, the cocaptain of the varsity cheerleading squad, had just texted her. *Wonder what she wants?* Haley thought, reading the message.

"Miller, sleepover at my house this weekend with Whitney and Coco. Your presence requested. Make that required. Make that, please don't leave me alone with the Cocobots. . . . xx Cecily." Haley snapped her phone shut and returned her attention to Reese.

"So," she said. "You've seen all our goofy snapshots from the Miller family road trips. Where are these Highlands-in-Europe pics I'm supposed to be looking at?"

"You sure you want to see them?" Reese asked, pulling a handsome leather-bound volume off the shelf behind the sofa. "They're pretty boring, if you ask me."

Of course the Highlands have tan leather photo albums that match their leather club chairs, Haley thought. *Of course.*

Haley looked at the artfully composed shots of Reese looking absolutely gorgeous in front of a series of French landmarks. "Did you hire a professional photographer to follow you around Paris?" she asked.

"It's sort of a hobby of my mom's," said Reese.

"Who's this?" Haley asked, pointing to an elegant Parisian woman who kept appearing in group shots. "She looks familiar."

"That's Sasha's mom," said Reese.

Haley knew that Mrs. Highland and Mrs. Lewis were old friends, and that they'd seen each other on the trip, but it was nevertheless an odd experience to actually see Sasha's mom staring back at her from the album, with Sasha's perfect bone structure and wide-set eyes.

"I can see the resemblance," said Haley.

"I wish Sasha could. She still refuses to have anything to do with her. When I tried giving her a letter her mom asked me to hand-deliver, she tore it up right in front of me."

"Well, I think Luke Lawson is now actually living with Sasha at the condo, and let's just say he's probably not the best influence on her. I saw them in the cafeteria together, just before the last theft."

"Maybe we should . . . ," Reese began.

"What? Tell our parents?" Haley asked. "I've thought about it myself. But what if they call the police and then Sasha ends up in foster care?"

"Well, I wasn't supposed to say anything, but the reason Sasha's mom moved back to France? She's been in med school. She just finished. While we were in Paris, she told us she's planning to move back to the U.S. and petition for custody at the end of the year."

"But maybe if your mom called her mom . . ."

"I'm sure she'd be on the next plane."

Barbara Highland appeared in the doorway in a navy blue apron and oven mitts, carrying the piping hot quiche.

"Dinner is served," Barbara said, setting the quiche down on the dining room table. Haley's mom emerged from the kitchen with a big bowl of salad and a cheese board piled high with white, yellow and orange wedges, along with a crusty baguette.

"What if Sasha doesn't want her mom's help?" Haley asked, looking at Reese.

"She'll come around," he said, taking her hand and pulling her up off the sofa. "She's got to. Trust me."

● ● ●

To have Haley and Reese TELL THE PARENTS about Sasha, go to page 167. Alternatively, you can send Haley to INVESTIGATE SASHA on her own (page 172). Finally, if you've had enough of the Sasha Lewis drama, have Haley go to CECILY WATSON'S HOUSE for a slumber party (page 159).

DOUBLE DATE

Double dates are often double the drama and half the fun.

Haley arrived at the local movie theater dressed in a blue pin-striped shirt, jeans and navy ballet flats—not exactly the ideal outfit for a hot date, but then, her parents had to give her the once-over before she walked out the door.

"Haley," Sebastian greeted her, sweeping her off her feet to give her a big hello kiss. Haley felt his stubble brush against her chin.

"Hello, Sebastian," she said, admiring his black trousers, which showed off his lean swimmer's build and his starched white cotton shirt, which, as usual, had the three top buttons undone. Haley thought he looked like he should be *on* a movie screen, not sitting in front of one.

By the time they reached the entrance of the theater, where Annie and Dave were waiting, Haley was so caught up in imagining what it would be like to kiss Sebastian that she almost didn't notice the miserable look on Annie's face.

Almost. Dave, too, Haley realized, seemed even more uncomfortable than usual.

The Moss is really taking a toll on their relationship, Haley thought, following Sebastian into the theater. "You okay?" she whispered to Annie while they waited in line for popcorn. Annie forced a brave smile and nodded, but Haley could see that no, in fact, her friend was not okay.

Sebastian found seats for the four of them at the back of the theater, positioning Haley so that she was between him and the wall. Dave was on the other side of Sebastian, sitting next to Annie, who was on the aisle.

"So what are we watching?" Haley asked as the lights dimmed. Until now, she'd been too distracted to ask.

"*Les Cousins Dangereux,*" said Sebastian. "It's French."

Great, Haley thought. *A sexy French film is not exactly what Dave and Annie need right now.* She looked over and saw that Dave was holding Annie's hand.

Then again, maybe a sexy French film is exactly what they need, Haley thought.

The first scene opened with a young girl taking a shower. Sebastian put his arm around Haley and gave her shoulder a squeeze.

"Popcorn?" Haley said, leaning across Sebastian and Dave to check on Annie. She handed the tub of popcorn to her friend.

"You okay?" Haley mouthed. Annie nodded.

"You know, Haley," Sebastian said, "in Spain, movies are not for eating."

"Oh?" Haley asked, looking up at him. She was now practically lying across his lap. Sebastian, who clearly liked seeing her in this position, began rubbing her shoulders.

Wow, Haley thought. *He's got really great hands. That feels amazing.*

"Relax," he whispered. "You Americans are so tense."

On the screen, the shower girl's mother knocked on the bathroom door. "Hannah," the woman called out. "Hannah?"

"*Oui, Maman?*" the pretty girl said, wrapping herself in a towel.

Uh-oh, Haley thought. *Did we have to pick a movie with Hannah as the lead?*

Haley heard a commotion at the end of the row and looked over just in time to see a visibly upset Annie rushing from the theater, with Dave chasing after her.

"Finally, we are alone together," Sebastian said, leaning closer to Haley.

"Wait," Haley said, pulling away and holding up a hand to stop him. *Annie might need me,* she thought, looking up at Sebastian's full lips, his square jaw, his dark seductive eyes. . . .

Then again, she thought, *this fight is clearly between Annie and Dave. Maybe I should just stay here with Sebastian and give them some space.*

● ● ●

What do you think Haley should do?

If you think she should catch up with Annie at the **ICE CREAM PARLOR** and make sure her friend is okay, turn to page 178. If you think **HALEY CAN'T RESIST** Sebastian and want Haley to let Dave and Annie handle their own problems anyway, turn to page 176.

HEAD TO CALIFORNIA

Sometimes it's best to leave the past behind you.

The flight to California was overbooked, so Haley ended up sitting in the back of the plane, squeezed between a chatty grandmotherly type and an overweight man who snored and spilled over into Haley's seat. She counted at least twenty packed rows separating her from Irene, Shaun and Devon, who were cozily seated together in an exit row toward the front of the plane.

Great, Haley thought. *What a way to start the vacation.*

The next five hours weren't exactly pleasant, as

Haley alternated between dodging the hefty man's drool, trying to get some sleep herself and politely answering the elderly woman's questions.

When the plane finally touched down at the San Francisco airport, Haley was exhausted and slightly disoriented. She disembarked to find that her friends weren't waiting for her at the gate as they had promised, but had already gone down to the baggage claim.

"Hi, Haley," Judy Waller greeted Haley briskly, with a cell phone pressed to her ear, as she collected her bags. "Gretchen had acting lessons, so she'll meet you at the house."

"Hi, Mrs. Waller," Haley said. What she was thinking was *Acting lessons? That's so not the Gretchen I remember.*

Without waiting for a response from Haley, Judy returned her attention to her cell phone. "I don't care if it's Friday afternoon, Charlie. Our presentation is Monday morning. We need those images by six a.m."

She's gotten much more intense since the last time I saw her, Haley thought, remembering that Mrs. Waller had gotten a big promotion the previous spring and was now a partner at her advertising agency.

Outside the terminal, Haley spotted Irene and the boys waiting in the line for a cab. "What happened to you guys?" Haley asked.

"Shaun got a little airsick midflight, so we had to get him outside as soon as the plane landed," Irene explained.

"Gosh, hope he feels better," Haley said, waving at Shaun, whose face was the color of split pea soup. He waved feebly back at her.

"We'd better get him to the hotel," Irene said.

"Okay. Call me tonight?" Haley said.

"Sure," Irene answered, working with Devon to situate Shaun in a cab.

Haley climbed into the Wallers' large, luxurious European sedan, which still had its new-car smell. "Gretchen didn't tell me you got a new car," Haley said to Mrs. Waller, who was plugging her phone into a headset so that she could talk and drive.

"Well, a lot has changed since you left, Haley," Mrs. Waller said.

"Like what?" Haley asked.

"You'll see."

The Wallers, like the Millers, had moved over the summer. But after selling their modest house in Marin County, they had relocated to San Francisco proper, where Mrs. Waller had inherited a Victorian row house from a favorite aunt who had died in a freak dog-walking accident.

"It's pretty big," Gretchen had warned Haley over the phone. Still, when Mrs. Waller pulled up the drive, Haley was stunned by its magnificence. The powder blue house was enormous and sat atop a hill with views of the water and the Golden Gate Bridge.

"Sorry I can't stay, but I have to go the office," Judy said, droppnig Haley off with a key. "Make yourself at home."

Easier said than done, Haley thought, staring up at the three-story mansion. Once inside, she was afraid to touch anything, so she sat gingerly on a pale yellow sofa in the parlor next to a perfectly trimmed Christmas tree and waited for Gretchen to come home.

She waited. And waited. And waited some more, occasionally dozing off for a few minutes here and there.

Almost an hour later, Gretchen finally breezed through the front door. At least Haley assumed it was Gretchen. Because this chick looked almost nothing like the girl Haley had left behind when she moved to New Jersey four months ago.

"Gretchen?" Haley gasped, eyeing the sleek black hair, oversized black sunglasses, black turtleneck, slim black capri pants and black slingback heels of her formerly mousy friend. "Who died?" Haley asked, assuming she'd just come from a funeral.

"Hey there," Gretchen said without taking off her sunglasses. "You look . . . exhausted. Those cross-country flights are the worst, aren't they?"

"Um, yeah," Haley said, wonderng when Gretchen had become bicoastal.

"Love the haircut. It suits you," said Gretchen.

"That's what my mom said," Haley whispered, almost too stunned to speak. Unlike the bubbly, almost ditzy old Gretchen, this one was aloof and much more sure of herself. At least she seemed that way.

"Shall we go up to my room?" Gretchen asked. Haley nodded and followed her up a grand staircase and into what looked like a formal guest bedroom with gleaming hardwood floors and deep red walls. "You can either stay in here with me or take the guest room," Gretchen said, adding, "But my room is much cozier."

Haley couldn't imagine anything more formal than the room she was now standing in, so she said, "I think I'll stay in here with you."

"There are fresh towels in the bathroom, and you can hang your things in the closet."

"So . . . you're taking acting lessons?" Haley asked tentatively.

"Yeah. It was the strangest thing. A casting agent came to our school and asked me to be in a commercial. As it turns out, I have a knack for it."

Haley felt ill. Who was this person, and what had she done with the old Gretchen? Instead of confronting her, she said, "So how's Harry?" referring to one of their oldest and closest friends.

"I wouldn't know. Since I moved into town, I haven't really kept up with old Harold," Gretchen said, using his full name. "That's what happens when you go to a new school," she added, with a fake-looking smile. "But not with us, of course. We'll *always* be friends. Won't we, Haley?"

Haley suddenly had a revelation: The new house, the new clothes, that gawd-awful black hair. Since

Haley had moved to New Jersey, Gretchen Waller had turned into Coco De Clerq. Haley wanted to grab her and scream, *"Wake up! Snap out of it!"*

"I think I'm going to take a hot shower and wash off the airplane funk," she said, hoping Gretchen was just going through a phase.

"Sure," Gretchen said, taking a script out of her—of course—black tote bag and sitting down on her antique chaise lounge. "I'll just be here, rehearsing my lines."

Haley locked herself in Gretchen's bathroom, turned on the tub faucet, took out her cell phone and immediately dialed Irene's number. *Come on, pick up,* she thought. But her call went straight to voice mail.

"Irene, it's Haley. Um, can you call me back?" Haley overheard Gretchen practicing her monologue in the next room. "It's an emergency," Haley said into the phone. "I need you pronto."

● ● ●

How did Gretchen go from being Haley's sweet, loveable pal to being a total snob in just four months? Or is Gretchen just putting up a front to hide the fact that she's struggling to fit into a new school and missing her old best friend?

What do you think Haley should do?

If you want her to confront Gretchen and save their friendship, turn to OLD FRIENDS (page 182). To have Haley disobey her parents and escape with Irene, Shaun and Devon, turn to NEW FRIENDS on page 188.

If people were meant to wear clothes, wouldn't we have been born in them?

Since the last thing Haley wanted to do was get wasted in a room full of boys, she decided to ante up with something else. At least then, she figured, she'd be alert enough to control what went on. The only problem was, her outfit wasn't exactly conducive to strip poker.

Why did I have to take off all those sweaters before I came here? she thought, wishing she hadn't stowed her extra layers in the bushes in front of her house. She decided to take off half of the only part of her ensemble she could spare: her high-heeled shoes.

"Ah-ah-ah. Shoes only count as a pair," Spencer pointed out.

"Like that's fair," Haley said, reluctantly letting her other shoe drop to the floor before tossing it into the pot.

For their antes, the boys all took bourbon shots. Coco took off her belt and tossed it to the center of the table. Whitney added her ribbon necklace.

At least I'm not the only one who doesn't have much on, Haley thought, glancing at Cecily in solidarity. *If we both end up naked, maybe we can huddle together for warmth.*

At that moment, Cecily pushed up the sleeves of her mohair sweater and revealed a stack of gold bangle bracelets at least two inches thick.

Ugh, I should've worn bling! Haley thought, suddenly terrified of what would happen next.

Spencer got up and walked over to Drew's computer. He turned on the speakers attached to the laptop, and an old Frank Sinatra song filled the room. "Now, it's basic five-card stud," he said as he returned to the table and reclaimed his seat. "You bet with a chip, that equals a shot."

Uh-oh, Haley thought, picking up her cards and discovering that all she had was a pair of fours and an ace. *Maybe I should just fold.*

Unfortunately, Spencer Eton must have been reading her mind. Looking directly at Haley, he said, "One final rule. There's a penalty clause if you fold. You automatically have to take a shot or take off

something else, since we wouldn't want people playing it too safe, now would we?"

"It's your bet, Haley," Coco said impatiently.

Haley considered her options. Now she would
have to take something else off even to exit the game,
so she might as well play out the hand. Right? *Here
goes nothing,* she thought, peeling off her purple top
and tossing it to the center of the dining room table
so that all she had on above the waist was a cream-
colored satin bra. *It's just like wearing a bikini, she
kept telling herself.*

Drew's jaw dropped. Spencer chewed the straw
from his drink. Toby politely averted his gaze. And
Matt just looked like he might burst.

"Come on, somebody say something," Haley said
self-consciously.

"Now we've got a party on our hands," Matt
replied, grinning ear to ear.

"Moving right along." Spencer signaled to Matt
that it was his turn to bet.

"Dude, how can I match that?" said Matt.

"You'll think of something," said Spencer.

Matt slid three of his chips in front of his hand.
Cecily tossed three bangles into the pot. Drew matched
with three chips, while Whitney took off her rabbit-
fur vest and set it on the table, revealing a tight
white see-through T-shirt, and under it, a black mesh
double-D-cup bra.

Coco glared at her.

"What?" Whitney said. "I was hot."

"Scorching," Drew nodded, staring at Whitney.

Toby shoved three chips forward. "I fold," Coco said defiantly, tossing her fedora into the pot. Spencer bet three chips, and suddenly it was Haley's turn again.

"I'll take two," she said, laying two of her cards facedown on the table. Spencer sent the new cards her way. Haley concentrated hard, willing them to be what she needed. She picked them up carefully.

Almost, she thought, looking down at the ace and the four she had just received. *A full house. That might just be good enough to win the hand, which means I'll get my clothes back. First I just have to figure out what to take off next.*

As everyone else refreshed their cards, Haley weighed her options. If she took off her skirt, she'd practically be naked, though only for a few minutes if she won the game. She could just take off her underwear and leave the skirt, though the thought of tossing her panties into the middle of the table seemed horribly wrong. The last option was to take off her bra, which she instantly ruled out.

Haley decided the skirt would be best. *It's just like a bikini,* she kept telling herself.

She stood up from the table and eased the skirt down over her hips, and over her turquoise bikini underwear. She stepped out of the skirt, then flung it onto the table.

Drew, only half kidding, said, "Haley, will you go to the prom with me?"

Whitney frowned. "Drew, only juniors and seniors can ask people to the prom. And besides, even if you could go, you should be asking me." Coco rolled her eyes.

One by one, everyone else folded except for Spencer and Matt.

"Call," said Haley, laying down her full house.

"Got me," said Spencer, who had two pair, kings high.

Haley reached into the center of the table to triumphantly collect her winnings. She was just about to put her purple top back on when Matt said, "Not so fast, sugar." He flipped over his hand to reveal four queens. Haley's stomach dropped. "It's too bad," Matt added, "because you look like you're catching cold."

Haley blushed, suddenly all too aware of how close to naked she actually was.

"Come on, man. Give her her clothes back," Toby said. He took off his jacket and handed it to Haley.

"If she couldn't handle the stakes, she shouldn't have agreed to play," said Matt, relishing his win.

Spencer got up and went back over to Drew's computer. He picked up a small silver object about the size of a deck of cards and slowly turned around. "Smile, Haley Miller," he said as she wrapped Toby's jacket around her bare shoulders. "How does it feel to be famous?"

What is that? Haley wondered, squinting to see

what Spencer was holding. *Is that . . . a camera?* She screamed and grabbed her skirt from Matt, scrambling to put it back on.

But it was too late.

● ● ●

Ouch. You really did Haley in this time.

Not only had Spencer recorded their little strip poker session, he'd streamed it live on the Internet. And as Haley would discover in the days, weeks, months and even years to come, once something's on the Internet, it stays on the Internet.

No matter how hard she and her parents tried to pull Spencer's footage off the Web, new versions and links kept popping up. Haley was teased about her starring role in "Hillsdale Hotties Play Strip Poker" all the way through high school. And college. And she was even accosted by a few of her "fans" while abroad in Europe one summer.

After that night at Drew Napolitano's, her life wasn't exactly ruined, but she had major trust issues to work out.

You blew it once again. Hang your head and go back to page 1.

DRINK AT SIGMA

At SIGMA, the shots are never cheap.

Looking down at her outfit, Haley saw that there was really nothing to take off that wouldn't reveal an embarrassing body part, except her shoes, and those wouldn't get her past the first hand.

"Here goes," she said, taking a full glass of champagne from Spencer and downing it before setting the empty glass back on the table. The boys all took bourbon shots as their ante, while Coco took off her belt and tossed it into the pot and Whitney added her ribbon necklace.

Great, Haley thought. *So far, I'm the only girl*

drinking. Well, at least Cecily is right here with me, she thought, looking at her friend in solidarity.

At that moment, Cecily pushed up the sleeves of her mohair sweater and revealed a two-inch thick stack of gold bangle bracelets. Haley groaned.

Ugh, should've known better than to leave the house without any bling, she thought.

"It's basic five-card stud," Spencer said while dealing. "Bet with chips or clothes. I don't care. Each chip represents one shot. At the end of the game, if you win, you get to make someone else drink. But if you lose, well, you have to take all the shots you bet, every one of them, by yourself."

I'm toast, Haley thought, picking up her cards and discovering that all she had was a pair of fours and an ace. *Maybe if I fold at the start of each game, I won't have to drink that much?*

But Spencer Eton must have been reading her mind, because he suddenly added, "One final rule. There's a penalty clause. If you fold, you automatically have to take another shot or take off something else. That's to keep people from playing it too safe."

Well, there goes that idea, Haley thought, just as the first wave of a champagne buzz hit her. Matt smiled at her, and Haley smiled back flirtatiously, suddenly emboldened by the alcohol. *Maybe this could be fun. Poker's not that hard. I just have to stay focused,* she thought.

Haley placed the first bet by sliding two chips in front of her hand.

"I like ambition in a woman," Matt said, matching the bet. Cecily followed by tossing two more bangles into the pot, and on the betting went, with the boys sliding chips in front of their hands, and the girls, except for Haley, shedding inconsequential accessories.

When it was her turn again, Haley placed two cards facedown on the table, closed her eyes and concentrated hard, willing the two she was dealt to be what she needed. She picked them up carefully.

Not bad, she thought, looking at the ace and the four she had just received. *A full house. That might just be good enough to win the hand.* She glanced down at the poker chips in front of her. Depending on how long the betting continued, she might be looking at five or six shots at stake.

Then again, if she folded now, she'd still have to drink the cup Spencer poured for her to exit the game. And, depending on who won, she still ran the risk of that person's reassigning shots for her to take.

Haley decided to go for it and slid two more chips into the center of the table. One by one, everyone else folded except for Spencer and Matt.

"Call," said Haley, laying down her full house.

"Got me," said Spencer, who had two pair, kings high.

Haley reached into the center of the table to triumphantly collect her winnings, but before she could Matt stopped her. "Not so fast, sugar," he said, flipping over his hand to reveal four queens. Haley's stomach dropped. Not only did she have to take the four shots she had bet, but Matt divvied up everyone else's chips and made each of the girls take one, including Haley.

When it came time to ante up for the second hand, Haley was noticeably tipsy. By round three, she was smashed. It wasn't until the start of the fifth game, though, that she ran to the powder room and started throwing up.

Cecily was nice enough to hold her hair back for her, and Toby and Matt alternated bringing her water.

As for Coco, Spencer, Drew and Whitney, they just kept playing. Until the following Monday at school, when they told everyone they knew about Haley's "calls to Ralph on the big white phone."

● ● ●

That little vomithon at SIGMA so wasn't cool.

Hang your head and go back to page 1.

CECILY WATSON'S HOUSE

Not everyone has
something to hide.

"Would you look at that—a perfect paperbark maple! Your father would freak out if he was here!" Joan Miller exclaimed as she pulled into the Watsons' gravel driveway.

"Hello," said Haley. "They own the Watson Nursery."

"You're kidding," Joan gasped, as if she couldn't imagine why she hadn't been told this earlier. "I've already placed an order with them for spring."

"I'll call you when I need to be picked up," Haley said, jumping out of the car before her mother could ask for an introduction to Cecily's parents. In Joan's eyes, these people were clearly celebrities.

"Haley!" Cecily said, greeting Haley at the door. "Sorry, I know this is sort of weird," she added, "but we're a no-shoes household."

"Hey, during planting season, so are we," said Haley, slipping off her cowboy boots and stepping inside.

"My mother is Hawaiian," Cecily explained. "It's one of their customs. Well, that, and she just hates vacuuming."

Haley followed her down the hall, which was decorated with fresh holiday wreaths.

"How did your mom end up in New Jersey?" Haley asked.

"Daddy was a navy man," said Cecily, leading Haley into the living room, past Japanese antiques made of ginkgo wood.

Coco was seated by the fireplace in the cozy den, next to the live fir tree adorned with white lights. She was surrounded by stacks of glossy magazines. "It's about time," she said as Haley entered.

Whitney was seated cross-legged on the floor, petting a white Persian cat on her lap.

"Aw. What's her name?" Haley asked, plopping down next to Whitney and the cat.

"This is Lo-Lo," Whitney said in a babyish voice.

"What does 'Lo-Lo' mean?" Haley asked, looking up at Cecily.

Cecily leaned in close and whispered, as if this

were something the cat was not supposed to hear: "It means dumb in Hawaiian. She has a little car-chasing problem. We can't let her out of the house."

"My kitty Princess Puffball looked just like her," Whitney said. "Oh, I miss the Wittle Princess."

Coco snickered.

"It's not funny, Coco," Whitney snapped, clutching the cat protectively.

"Why don't you tell them what happened to Princess Puffball?" Coco said. "Whitney thinks her cat was *taken advantage of* by a stray."

"Taken advantage of?" Cecily asked.

"She had five illegitimate kittens," Whitney said, all too seriously. "And Princess Puffball was not a cat who would do that sort of thing."

"Whitney, Princess was not attacked by a tomcat," Coco said. "She was just easy."

Cecily couldn't help herself and started laughing. Soon Haley was cracking up too.

"I'm sorry," Cecily said, regaining her composure.

"So what happened to the kittens?" Haley asked, biting her lip. "And Princess Puffball?"

"Our cleaning lady found homes for the little babies," said Whitney. "And Princess Puffball was sent to the country where she couldn't get into any more trouble."

"Wait a minute," said Cecily. "Whitney, who cleans your house?"

"Flavia," Whitney said, still petting Lo-Lo. "Why?"

"Um, Whitney, I don't know how to tell you

this," Cecily began, "but I think Lo-Lo might be one of Princess Puffball's long-lost kittens. We got her from a woman named Flavia."

"No way!" Whitney said, holding Lo-Lo up to her face. "Aw, if I'd known you were going to be this cute, I never would've let my daddy give you away." She gave Lo-Lo an Eskimo kiss, and then began rocking the cat back and forth like an infant.

"Cecily?" Mrs. Watson called from the kitchen. "You have a telephone call."

"Who is it?" Cecily asked.

"A boy named Reese Highland."

Haley felt queasy. *What's Reese doing calling Cecily?* she wondered.

"Isn't that interesting," Coco said, watching Haley's reaction.

Cecily got up and went to take the call in the next room.

"Well, that's a relief," Coco whispered in a confiding tone to Haley. "I was starting to think Reese didn't like girls."

"What's that supposed to mean?" Haley asked, trying to sound nonchalant.

"Well, he rejected you, didn't he?" Coco said slyly. "I mean everyone knows you've got, like, this huge crush on him. And he's never done the first thing about it."

You're one to talk, Haley thought, clenching her teeth.

"I guess he was just waiting for the right girl to

come along," said Coco. "I mean, ever since your slumber party, he hasn't stopped talking about Cecily. And to think, those two kids have you to thank for bringing them together."

Haley was practically fuming when Cecily returned from the kitchen, carrying a tray of fresh fruit.

"So?" Coco prodded immediately. "What did Mr. Highland want?"

Haley waited anxiously for Cecily's response.

"Just a phone number," said Cecily, setting the tray down on the coffee table.

"Whose?" Haley blurted out. She cleared her throat and added, "I mean, whose number did he want?"

Coco smiled triumphantly, satisfied that she had finally rattled Haley Miller.

"Our neighbors own a limousine service. He needed to book a car," Cecily said.

"Oh," said Haley, relaxing enough to bite into a slice of pineapple. "That's all," she said, glancing at Coco.

"So Reese is ordering a limo?" Coco said, arching an eyebrow.

"Ooooh, maybe it's for your birthday," Whitney said, clapping her hands together and nearly dropping Lo-Lo on her head. "Maybe he's planning to pick you up in it and take you to the party? Wouldn't that be awesome?"

"My parents have already taken care of that," said Coco. "They've taken care of everything."

Haley knew she wasn't kidding. In fact, everyone in Hillsdale was aware of Coco De Clerq's impending sixteenth birthday. Her parents had made sure of that. They were planning a huge party at the local country club to celebrate, and all the kids at Hillsdale High were clamoring for an invite.

"Actually," Cecily said, "Reese said it was for an airport pickup. Sasha's mom is flying into Newark next week."

"Sasha's mother? Coming back to Hillsdale?" Whitney said, stunned. "Coco, did you know about this?"

Haley instantly realized the answer to that question was a big fat no.

"Well, just wait until Mrs. Lewis sees what a freak her daughter has turned into," Coco muttered. "She'll be on the next flight back to Paris." Coco picked up a magazine and began angrily flipping through it.

Haley was enjoying the fact that it was now Coco who was rattled.

Out of habit, Whitney picked up a magazine and copied Coco. "Do you think she would dare show up at your party?" Whitney asked, absently.

"Why would Mrs. Lewis want to go to Coco's party?" Haley asked.

"No, dummy. Sasha," said Whitney. It was rare that Whitney got the chance to make someone else look foolish, so she took great pleasure in rubbing it in. "Duh."

"I've given her photo to security," said Coco. "Sasha won't be setting foot within a hundred yards of the club that night. And neither will her skeevy boyfriend, Johnny Lane."

Haley could hardly believe that just two months ago, Sasha had been one of Coco and Whitney's best friends. *So much for loyalty,* she thought, realizing that at any moment, they might turn on her too.

"Maybe you should have these at your sweet sixteen," Whitney said, holding up a magazine photo of a colorful floral arrangement.

"Birds of paradise?" said Cecily. "Somehow that doesn't quite seem like Coco's style."

"Would you just make up your mind already?" Whitney said. "I can't plan my outfit until I know your theme."

"I'm glad you mentioned it," said Coco. "Starting Monday, study hall will now be dedicated to planning my party." She looked at Cecily and Haley, warning them with her gaze that skipping was definitely not an option.

Guess I can always study at home, Haley thought at first. Then she frowned. *Since when did I sign up for the Coco De Clerq mafia?* She wondered, suddenly filled with the urge to disobey Coco and reclaim her life.

● ● ●

If you think Haley's had enough of Coco for one life-time, turn to SASHA'S MOM ARRIVES on page 202. If you want her to be involved with Coco's spectacular sweet sixteen gala, turn to PARTY PLANNER on page 196.

Remember, Coco wasn't asking. There will be penalties for disobeying her command—like not getting an invite to the party of the school year.

TELL THE PARENTS

Parents usually mean it when they say you can tell them anything.

"**M**om, Dad, Mr. and Mrs. Highland, Reese and I have something to tell you," Haley said. As Reese took her hand, Joan Miller's face went sheet-white.

"You're not pregnant, are you?" Joan asked.

Haley turned bright red. "Mom! Of course not."

"Marcus. Would. Like. A nephew," Mitchell said, looking up at Haley.

"Well, Marcus isn't getting one," said Haley. "Not for a long, long time."

"It's our friend Sasha," said Reese.

"Is she pregnant?" Perry asked.

"No, Dad," said Haley.

"She's in trouble, though," said Reese.

"Oh, thank goodness," Joan blurted out. She quickly added in a concerned tone, "I mean, what's wrong with Sasha? What sort of trouble is she in?"

"We think her dad might have a problem," Reese began.

"With gambling. And alcohol," Haley added.

"He disappeared a few weeks ago, and Sasha's been . . ." Reese hesitated.

"What is it, son?" his father asked.

"She's been living on her own at the condo ever since."

"With this guy from school named Luke," Haley added. "He's not exactly a good influence. I mean, I know he's been arrested. At least once."

"I'm glad you came to us," Mrs. Highland said. "It was the right thing to do. I only wish you'd said something sooner." She hurried into the kitchen to find her address book and called Sasha's mom.

Oliver put on his coat and grabbed his car keys.

"Where are you going?" Reese asked.

"Sasha can stay with us until her mother arrives," Mr. Highland said.

"I'll go with you," said Perry, following him out the door.

Joan Miller remained in the dining room, looking at Haley and Reese. "How long have you two known about this?"

"Not long," said Haley.

"But obviously since before today."

Reese and Haley exchanged glances. "Reese had no idea," Haley said. "I was afraid if I said anything, Sasha would end up in foster care. It wasn't until Reese mentioned her mom that it seemed like there might be a way to help."

"You should've told us what was going on from the start," said Joan. "If nothing else, we could've given her a place to stay until we figured out what to do."

"Don't you think I offered? She didn't want our help."

Haley's mom raised her voice. "Haley, if the situation is as out of control as you say it is, it's not for Sasha to decide whether or not she wants our help. She's fifteen years old. What if something had happened to her? What if she's already in over her head?"

Haley bit her lip. The gravity of the situation hadn't really hit her until now.

"Sasha's a good kid, Mrs. Miller," said Reese. "I'm sure she'll be okay."

"I. Am. Hungry," Mitchell said, poking his mom with his wooden coat hanger.

"I know you are, sweetheart," said Joan, "but we have to wait for Daddy to get back." She carried the quiche back into the kitchen to keep it warm in the oven.

Reese turned to Mitchell. "What do you say

you and me go play video games until supper? Huh, buddy?"

"Affirmative," said Mitchell, following Reese down the hall.

They paused at the door to the study and Reese added, "Haley, you coming?"

She smiled halfheartedly. Just as she was about to join them, her cell phone vibrated. This time, the text was from Coco De Clerq.

"Hey you . . . I need your help. Meet me in study hall on Monday to discuss. Ciao. Coco."

That's weird, Haley thought. *Text messages from two different masters of the universe in a single day. Since when did I become the latest candidate for Miss Popularity?*

"C'mon, Miller, get a move on," Reese called out. "We've got a sea monster to beat."

"Coming," Haley said as she wandered down the hall past the perfectly symmetrical, but as yet undecorated, Christmas tree in a daze.

● ● ●

Well, that's a load off Haley's mind. Finally, Sasha will be able to get the help she needs. But now that Sasha's out of the woods, will Reese and Haley finally be able to be together? Or will something come between them once again?

To see what happens when SASHA'S MOM ARRIVES, turn to page 202. If you think Haley should find out what Coco wants, turn to PARTY PLANNER on page 196.

With just a few weeks left in the semester, a lot can happen to our Haley. Depending on which way you choose, she could end up with everything she's ever wanted, or squandering her one real chance at happiness. Then again, if there's one thing Haley's good at, it's changing her mind.

INVESTIGATE SASHA

Trouble is never
that hard to find.

Haley knew Sasha needed help. But she was afraid if she went to her parents and told them what was going on, they might feel the need to contact the police. Haley knew that could land Sasha in a foster home, at least until her father resurfaced and got himself clean, or her mother turned up.

Then again, she knew if she did nothing, Sasha might end up seriously hurt, or at least in a worse place than foster care.

It was all so confusing, Haley was starting to lose sleep at night.

She finally decided that, before she made any concrete decisions, she would need to investigate.

Which is how Haley Miller came to be wearing a black hooded sweatshirt and dark glasses, following Sasha Lewis through the school parking lot in the middle of a Thursday afternoon.

Sasha was carrying a brown paper bag and looking furtively over her shoulder. Haley had to duck behind cars to avoid being seen.

As Sasha climbed into Luke Lawson's van, Haley began to worry she might lose them. But miraculously, she spotted a taxi waiting in front of the school in the loading zone. She hopped into the backseat and said, "Follow that van."

"Are you for real, kid?" the taxi driver said, shaking his head.

"Just follow them! Please!" Haley said urgently.

"Kid, if your name isn't Hannah Moss, I ain't taking you anywhere," the driver said.

"Sir, please. Can't you call the dispatcher and have them send another cab?"

"Look, kid—"

"I'll give you twenty bucks," Haley offered.

"Don't do me any favors," said the driver, chuckling.

"Twenty-five."

The driver stared at her in the rearview mirror.

"Thirty," Haley said, "but that's my final offer."

"What is it, Nancy Drew, your boyfriend stepping out on you?" he asked.

Haley shook her head. "Trust me. It's bigger than that."

"Okay, kid. But this meter goes past thirty bucks and I'm dropping you off on the curb, no matter where we are."

He radioed for another cab to be sent to the school and stepped on the gas, pulling into traffic a few cars lengths behind the van.

Thirty bucks? Haley thought. *I can't afford that.*

Just then, her cell phone vibrated. She ducked down, wondering if Sasha had caught sight of her, but the text was from Coco De Clerq.

"Hey you . . . I need your help. Meet me in study hall on Monday to discuss. Ciao. Coco."

She's probably just trying to finalize the guest list for her silly sweet sixteen party, Haley thought. *She has no idea what a real problem is.*

The taxi followed Luke's van to a run-down house in the Floods with a sagging front porch and peeling gray paint. Luke left the van running, got out and nodded to Sasha, who followed him into the house, still carrying the brown paper bag.

"You know those kids?" the taxi driver asked Haley.

"Yeah," she said.

"Well, stop knowing them."

"Why?" Haley asked.

"They deal drugs in that house."

Haley felt queasy. *Sasha, mixed up with drugs?*

she thought. *Maybe I should have gone straight to my parents. Or to the police.*

"Look, you seem like a nice kid," the driver said. "There's no use in you messing around with those type people. Keep your nose clean."

"It's the girl I'm worried about," Haley said. "She's nice, too. At least she used to be."

"Listen," he explained, "ain't nobody nice goes into that house. And even if they was nice when they went in, they ain't when they come out. Got me?" Haley had a sinking feeling the driver was right.

● ● ●

If you think it's too late for Sasha, send Haley straight to the police to TURN HER IN on page 207. Alternatively, you can find out what happens when SASHA'S MOM ARRIVES on page 202. Finally, see what Coco wants in PARTY PLANNER on page 196.

There's only so much you can do for a friend in need, particularly when that friend is hanging out with a bad seed like Luke Lawson. Make that Law-less. Is it really Haley's responsibility to save Sasha from herself? Then again, if Haley doesn't help her, who will?

HALEY CAN'T RESIST

One little kiss won't hurt.
Or will it?

Within minutes, Haley had forgotten all about Annie and Dave and their silly little squabbles. She let Sebastian raise the armrest separating their seats, and soon he had one hand on the small of her back, while the other was massaging her knee. Haley felt his breath against her neck as he kissed his way up to her mouth, pausing to nibble on her ear. She was nervous at first, but Sebastian had a way of calming her down.

However, after several minutes of making out, Haley suddenly became aware of something more than a blush on her face. A distinct burning sensation snapped her back to reality, and she began to wonder what she was doing feverishly making out with a hairy, manly foreign exchange student in the back row of her local theater.

What am I doing? Haley thought, stealing a look around the darkened space to see if she recognized anyone. *This is such a bad idea.*

● ● ●

To keep Haley making out with Sebastian, turn to STUBBLE TROUBLE (page 209). To cut the date short and catch up with Annie at school the following day, turn to PATCHWORK (page 210).

The best way to get over being dumped? Take two gallons of ice cream and don't call him in the morning.

After excusing herself and leaving Sebastian alone at the theater, Haley finally found Annie drowning her sorrows in a gigantic sundae at the ice cream parlor near the movie theater. Dave was nowhere in sight.

"He dumped me, Haley," Annie moaned when Haley walked in. "Can you believe it? He actually dumped me."

"What happened?" Haley asked gently.

"He said I'm paranoid. *Me*, paranoid," Annie said incredulously, picking at the mounds of pistachio, cherry and mint chocolate chip ice cream doused with hot fudge sauce and whipped cream.

"Why would he think that?" Annie asked.

"Tell me exactly what happened," said Haley. "And don't leave anything out."

"I accused him of cheating on me with Hannah Moss."

"And what did he say?" Haley asked.

Annie sighed. "That nothing was going on, that it was all in my head."

"Well, do you think that maybe he has a point—"

"It's not, Haley. It is *not* in my *head*." Annie began sobbing, with huge tears following the already tear-stained paths on her cheeks. "And the worst part is, he's going to Coco's. With Hannah. On my birthday!" Annie wailed. "It couldn't have happened any better if Coco De Clerq had planned it herself."

"Slow down. What are you talking about?" Haley asked, taking one of Annie's napkins and dabbing her eyes.

"Coco . . . and I . . . have the same . . . birthday," Annie said, practically hyperventilating. "We used to be best friends. Did you know that? We celebrated every year together with a joint party, until . . ."

"What?" Haley asked.

"Until the third grade, when I . . ."

"Go on," Haley coaxed.

Annie shook her head. "It doesn't matter," she said. "Coco just suddenly stopped wanting to be friends with me. But she kept having parties and inviting everyone in our grade except for me.

"Somehow that doesn't surprise me," said Haley.

"No one ever came to my birthdays, Haley. Once I even tried moving my party to a different day. But Coco changed hers, too. She invited everyone up to her parents' place in the Catskills. The De Clerqs rented vans and everything."

Haley was horrified. "That's just evil," she said. "So what does all this have to do with Dave and Hannah?"

"Well," Annie began. "You know how Hannah does all the sound engineering for Rubber Dynamite? Well, they're playing at Coco's party. Hannah asked Dave if he could help, and"—Annie began sobbing again—"h-h-he, he, he said yes."

Haley sat still for a moment, taking in all this information. "Well, did he know it was your birthday too?" she asked, patting her friend's hand.

"H-h-how could he not know my birthday?"

"Well, it's like you said," Haley began, "if Coco's birthday always dominates the month of December, maybe he really and truly didn't know. I'm sure if you just explain the situation to him—"

Annie shook her head. "He said he'd promised Hannah he would help, and that he can't go back on his word. So once again, Coco's ruined my birthday, only this time it's my sweet sixteen." Annie put her head down on the table and quietly gasped for breath.

Haley had no idea what to do to make her friend feel better.

"Once he's had a chance to think things over, I'm sure he'll figure out a way to get out of helping Hannah. Then the four of us—you, Dave, me and Sebastian—will make up for all those years you didn't have a party."

Annie sniffled. "You really think so?"

"I know so," said Haley, hoping against hope she was right. *And if not,* Haley thought, *believe me, Annie, I'll make Coco De Clerq regret every terrible thing she's ever done to you.*

● ● ●

To do a little PATCHWORK and fix things between Annie and Dave, turn to page 210. To CONFRONT COCO and find out why she's tortured Annie for all these years, turn to page 217.

Is it any wonder Annie Armstrong turned out the way she did, after seven years of suffering at the hands of the schemy Coco De Clerq? Can any punishment fit this crime? And if so, is Haley crafty enough to pull it off? Read on to find out.

There aren't too many people in this world who remember what you look like in diapers.

While Haley was sitting in Gretchen's bathroom waiting for Irene to call her back, she began to see how rude it would be to duck out on the Wallers on her first night in town. They were, after all, letting her stay with them, even though it clearly wasn't a convenient time for Mrs. Waller. Haley thought of how offended she would be if Gretchen came to New Jersey and disappeared with a bunch of people she'd never met.

Too, Haley wanted to figure out what was going on with her friend. Before Haley and her family had left for New Jersey, Gretchen Waller had been the sweetest, most easygoing, most fun-loving girl in Marin County. Now she seemed like just another city brat in high heels.

Haley sent another text to Irene, letting her know the emergency had passed and suggesting that they all meet up in the morning so that Haley could introduce Irene and the boys to Gretchen. After a quick shower, she combed her hair and went out to face Gretchen.

Haley found her sitting on a chaise, looking over her script. Haley plopped down on the bed. "Don't you need a partner to run lines?" she asked.

Gretchen looked up, surprised. "Are you offering?" she asked.

"Sure, why not," said Haley. "It's just acting. How hard can it be?"

Gretchen smirked and pulled another copy of the script from her bag. "Okay. You read Reginald. I'll be Ainsley."

Reginald and *Ainsley*? Haley thought. *What are we reading, an eighteenth-century soap opera?*

Gretchen sensed Haley's hesitation. "It's our assignment for the week," she said. "We have to act out a scene written by a fellow student."

"Ah," said Haley. "Let's hope there are better actors than writers in the drama department."

"Our coach says the hardest thing to do in this craft is to act well in bad material."

Haley looked down at her script so that Gretchen wouldn't see her rolling her eyes. *Whatever happened to just doing Shakespeare like everyone else?* she wondered.

"Look, if you don't want to do this—" Gretchen said.

"No, no, no. I'm in, Gretch"—Haley deepened her voice and added an over-the-top British accent— "or should I say . . . Ainsley?"

"Haley!" Gretchen protested, but Haley continued in character.

"By my troth, thy Reginald is at thy service." Haley raised an eyebrow and looked up, expecting to see Gretchen giggling. Instead, her friend's face was still frozen in anger. "Oh, come on," Haley said. "Not even a smile?"

"I take my work very seriously."

Haley frowned. "Yeah, you seem to be taking everything pretty seriously these days."

"What's that supposed to mean?" Gretchen asked.

"It means I've only been gone for a few months, and I come back and you're a *Totally. Different. Person*. The house, the clothes, the new school . . . the hair."

Gretchen looked hurt. "You think I chose all this?" she asked.

"Whether or not you chose it, you certainly seem to be enjoying it."

"My mom got a promotion, Haley. We inherited the house. It made sense for us to move into the city. But no one ever asked me how I felt about it. Not once. Since you left, do you think anyone's asked me how I've felt about *anything*?"

It was good to finally see Gretchen show some real emotion, even if she was breaking down. "So that's why you're wearing black and taking acting lessons?" Haley asked.

"You don't understand what it's like at that school, what the people are like at Avondale Academy. The other kids have all known each other since preschool. The girls don't wear anything unless it has a designer label in it. The cafeteria serves poached salmon with lemon dill sauce and potato *rösti* for lunch. And in class, we have to call each other Ms. Waller and Mr. Whitaker."

"Welcome to my worst nightmare," said Haley.

"I told you." Gretchen looked away.

"So quit. Go to public school, like me."

"My parents don't want me attending public school in the city. It's not up for debate."

"But if it's that unbearable, Gretchen—"

Gretchen shrugged. "Some days it's not. I started taking lessons because the drama kids are left alone at school. But then I actually started to like it. I even think I might be good at it."

"All I know is I miss my best friend."

"Me too." Gretchen's eyes misted over. "I wish you still lived here."

Haley sighed. "Haven't you made any new friends yet?"

Gretchen blushed. "Well, there is this one guy. . . ."

"Let me guess," said Haley. "Mr. Whitaker?" Gretchen nodded. "Well, tell you what. Why don't we order takeout from the Thai Palace, braid our hair, and you can tell me all about him."

"Just like old times?" Gretchen asked with a grin.

"Just like old times," said Haley.

"I'll go get menus," Gretchen said, bounding down the stairs. While Haley was still waiting for her to return, her cell phone vibrated.

Messages, she thought. *Probably Irene begging me to save her from being alone with the boys.*

But it wasn't Irene's voice. "Hi, Haley, it's Mom. Just wanted to make sure you got in okay and are having a good time. Oh, and to let you know that an invitation just arrived for you. It was hand-delivered. The messenger said something about Coco De Clerq's birthday party? Anyway, be safe. Say hello to the Wallers. And call me when you have a minute. Love you."

Haley pressed Save and played her next message. "Hey, Red." It was Reese Highland. Haley nearly fell off the bed. "When are you getting back from San Francisco? I was thinking maybe we could have dinner this weekend and catch up? Anyway. Call me."

No way, she thought. *Did Reese Highland just ask me out?*

"So what'll it be, Miller?" Gretchen asked, arriving

in the doorway holding the Thai Palace menu and a cordless phone. "Pad Thai, green chicken curry, papaya beef salad?"

But Haley was too lost in her own thoughts to respond.

● ● ●

If you think Haley should pack her stuff and head home to New Jersey sooner rather than later, send her on that DATE WITH REESE (page 241), or to COCO'S SWEET SIXTEEN (page 262). Alternatively, if you want her to stay in California and see what happens when old friends and new come together, turn to WORLDS COLLIDE on page 220.

NEW FRIENDS

**You find out a lot
about people when you
travel together. Sometimes
too much.**

Haley got tired of waiting for Irene to call her back. So she decided to go find her friends at the hotel. First, all she had to do was break the news to Gretchen.

"You know," Haley said, hopping out of the shower and wrapping herself in a towel as she hastily grabbed a pair of jeans and a sweater from her bag, "I should probably check on Irene and the boys. They know nothing about San Francisco. You can come with me if you like, though I doubt it would be much fun since they're probably going to want to do a lot of touristy stuff."

Gretchen stiffened. "I have an audition in the morning," she said.

"Well, I mean, if you're sure, we can always meet up with you later."

"No thanks. Go find your friends," said Gretchen. "I'll cover for you if your mom calls."

Haley thought she detected the slightest note of disappointment in Gretchen's voice, and was about to change her mind when Gretchen suddenly added, "Besides, aren't they all from, like, *New Jersey*? Why would I want to hang out with them?"

"Like I said," Haley replied, controlling her temper, "I doubt it would be much fun for you." She couldn't help adding, "So what's the audition for, anyway? Another *commercial*?"

Gretchen gave her a dirty look. "Like my acting teacher says, you have to hone your instrument before you can really use it."

"Riiiiight," Haley said in a patronizing tone. "See ya," she said, grabbing her bags and heading downstairs. By the time she reached the front door, there was a taxi waiting for her, with Irene, Shaun and Devon in the backseat.

"Hoss, you said it was an emergency," Shaun explained.

"You sounded a little desperate," Irene added.

Thank goodness, Haley thought. *I don't think I could stand another minute with Gretchen's "instrument."* She climbed into the cab. Irene was wearing a kelly green shirtdress with a white collar and the name

Suzi embroidered on the breast pocket, and black lace-up ankle boots.

Shaun had on his usual faded black jeans with a chain attached to his belt, a black T-shirt and an orange plaid derby cap that seemed to be his new purchase for the day.

And Devon was wearing a cool tweed blazer, a green T-shirt, jeans and, of course, his 35 mm camera. He looked, Haley thought, all in all, pretty cute.

"So I see you three hit the thrift stores without me," Haley said. "That must mean Shaun's feeling better."

"Like peas and carrots," Shaun said. "Seriously, I want some peas, carrots, fried chicken, ice cream."

"Believe it or not," Irene said, "Shaun's hungry."

"Well, sugar, what'd you expect? Shouting at my shoes left me a pizza-sized hole right about . . . here." He pointed to a spot on the left side of his stomach and, on cue, it growled.

"Dude, how is it you have a cast-iron stomach on land, but the minute you're airborne, you get motion sick?" Devon asked.

"I got a don't ask, don't tell policy with my pie safe," Shaun said, holding his gut. "I don't ask why it gets angry, and it don't tell me to stop."

"So where should we eat?" Haley asked.

"You're the native," said Devon. "Isn't that why we brought you? You're our tour guide on this trip."

"What do you mean 'native,' Oregon? I see it didn't take you long to reassimilate to the West Coast," she said. "You look like you were plucked out of Portland this morning."

"It is good to be back out here," he said, breathing in the San Francisco air.

Well, he's certainly more relaxed than he has been in Hillsdale, Haley thought. *Maybe this trip was just what he needed.*

"Yeehaw, let's crack this city open like a cockleshell," Shaun squealed.

"Translation," said Irene. "The Shaun now wants seafood."

"Well, what the Shaun wants . . . ," Haley began.

"The Shaun most definitely gets," said Devon.

"I think I know just the place," Haley said. She leaned into the front seat and whispered an address in the cabbie's ear. He drove down a few side streets and dropped them off in front of an alleyway that led to a tiny old crab shack with low ceilings and a small carved wooden man in blue rain gear guarding the door.

"Welcome to the Fisherman's Dwarf," said Haley. "King crab legs, Alaskan salmon, Washington State oysters, and did I mention it's all-you-can-eat?"

"Excellent," Shaun said, nodding in approval as he looked around.

"Clearly, you know what Shaun likes," said Devon.

"It's not that hard," said Haley. "Dwarves and portions that come by the pound."

Two hours and eight helpings of peel-and-eat shrimp later, they wandered back to the hotel.

"You sure you don't want to come upstairs with us?" said Irene.

"There's plenty of room," said Devon. "Shaun's parents booked us a suite."

Haley was tempted. "There's a pool," Devon added. "We could take a little midnight swim."

"We got us a minibar," said Shaun. "You know what that means, boozing little people. Woo hoo, I'm catching me a leprechaun this trip."

"You should see the traps he left out," Devon said, winking at Haley.

"If the cocktail wieners don't nab 'em, the non-parallels will," said Shaun.

"How long is this Lilliputian obsession of yours going to last?" Irene said.

"Dude, it's anthropomorphology," said Shaun. "Any of you cats know the life span of a hobbit?"

"I should get back to Gretchen's," said Haley.

Devon looked disappointed. "Really?"

"My parents were gracious enough to let me come on this trip, but if they catch me spending the night at a hotel with boys, I won't be allowed to cross the New Jersey state line again until I'm eighteen."

"Bummer," said Shaun. "Guess that means no pool party. I don't take my clothes off unless there are at least two females present." He grabbed Haley and Irene in a double headlock.

"Why don't we all hang out tomorrow?" Haley offered. "I can show you around. You guys can finally meet Gretchen."

"Are you sure the young Meryl Streep can get away from her audition?" Irene asked sarcastically.

Shaun belched loudly and said, "Leave the stuck-up thespian to me, hoss. I'll unloosen her right up."

"I'm afraid if she meets you, she'll get wound even tighter," said Haley.

"You and your lady friend just meet us in front of the SFMOMA at eight in the a.m.," said Shaun.

"Isn't that a little early for the MOMA?" Haley asked.

"The moms and pops booked us on a little listening parade," said Shaun.

"We're getting a private guided tour of the museum," said Irene. "They do that sort of thing for donors. Big donors."

"Well, that'll certainly impress Gretchen."

"Don't you mean Wretched?" Devon asked.

"Very funny. She's still my oldest friend."

"Oldest and queerest," said Irene.

"Aw, yeah, we're going Ferris Bueller all over San Fran," Shaun said, taking Irene by the hand. Irene grabbed the hand of a little blond kid who was milling around by the valet station with his twin sister. The kid grabbed his sister's hand, and she grabbed the hand of the valet. The five of them circled the fountain in front of the hotel as Shaun provided a soft lyrical accompaniment by humming an old tune by the Smiths.

Devon, meanwhile, pulled Haley aside. "Sorry we weren't able to sit together on the plane," he said.

"Well, neither one of us was really in a position to complain, considering we're both here on free tickets."

Devon smiled. "And to think, I almost didn't come."

"I'm glad you did," said Haley.

"Me too," he said. "Look, I know I've been acting sort of weird lately."

"Really?" Haley teased. "I hadn't noticed."

"It's just, it hasn't been easy, losing my scholarship. And I guess I've been taking it out on the people around me."

"We all know you're going through a lot right now," said Haley. "But you have to look at the bright side."

"What's that?" said Devon.

"Now you're in school with all of us." He smiled. "You know the art program at Hillsdale really isn't all that bad," she added. "Though it helps if you have talent."

"You'll figure out what your talent is," Devon assured her. "Sooner or later." He kissed her goodnight on the cheek and put her into a cab. She waved to Irene and Shaun, who was now floating on his back in the middle of the fountain, fully clothed. The twins were staring at him as if he was their new hero.

Haley's cell phone began to vibrate as the cabbie pulled out of the parking lot. *Messages,* she thought. *That's probably Gretchen wondering where I am.*

Haley dialed her voice mail, but it wasn't Gretchen.

"Hi, Haley, it's Mom. Just wanted to make sure

you got in okay and are having a good time. Oh, and to let you know that an invitation just arrived for you. It was hand-delivered. The messenger said something about Coco De Clerq's birthday party? Anyway, be safe out there. Say hello to the Wallers. And call us to check in when you have a minute. Love you."

Haley pressed Save and listened to her next message. "Hey, Red." It was Reese Highland. "When are you getting back from San Francisco? I was thinking maybe we could have dinner this weekend and catch up? Anyway. Call me."

No way, she thought. *Did Reese Highland just ask me out?*

●　●　●

Since when did it start raining boys in Hillsdale? Maybe the better question is, why has it taken this long for everyone to finally notice Haley Miller?

Reese must have some serious intuition, leaving Haley that voice mail right as Devon was making his move. But then, absence does make the heart grow fonder, right?

If you think Haley should pack her stuff and head home to New Jersey sooner rather than later, send her on that DATE WITH REESE (page 241), or send her to COCO'S SWEET SIXTEEN (page 262). Alternatively, if you want her to stay in California and see what happens when old friends and new come together, turn to WORLDS COLLIDE on page 220.

Some invitations you just
don't want to get.

Per Coco's instructions, Haley showed up in the library just as the bell for fifth period sounded. The only problem was, Coco, Whitney and Cecily were nowhere to be found.

Haley set her books down on one of the wooden tables and went looking for them in the stacks. *They better not have cut,* she thought, wandering toward the mystery thriller section.

She heard whispers coming from the shelves, and followed the sound of voices.

I should so be studying for my next math test, she thought.

Sure enough, Coco, Whitney and Cecily were lounging on an old leather sofa near the fire escape.

"You call this studying?" Haley said in a stern voice.

"Oh, hi," Coco said, and quickly closed the blue binder on her lap.

"Hey, Haley," Cecily said, looking slightly guilty.

"So," Haley said, "how's the party planning?"

"Great," Whitney said.

"Brilliant," Coco added.

"It's going to be some party," Cecily said, nodding in agreement.

"I'm sure it is," said Haley, wondering what they'd been talking about before she arrived.

"There's still a ton to do," Coco said, looking down the aisles to make sure a librarian wasn't going to interrupt their meeting. "Only the first draft picks are completed. But that's the easy part. The A-list is, after all, always the A-list. It's inviting the wannabes that gets complicated."

"I have an idea," Whitney suggested. "We could hold a lottery. A loser lottery."

"I never thought I'd say this to you, Whitney, but . . . good idea," Coco said.

Whitney basked in the glow of Coco's approval.

"What's a loser lottery?" Haley asked.

"Coco came up with it in eighth grade," Whitney explained. "We cut up an old yearbook and take out all the pictures of kids we would only ever say hi to if they were the only other person in a room. And then we put those pictures in a pile facedown and we pick out the lucky losers."

"So let me get this straight. You're inviting people you don't like to your birthday party?" Haley asked Coco in disbelief.

"Every epic production needs a few extras," Coco said, glancing back at her.

"Besides, most of them just stand there worshiping us," Whitney said. "And it never hurts to have a little ASP."

"ASP?" Haley asked.

"Attention Surplus Party," said Whitney. "It's like a spa day for the psyche."

"Riiiight," Haley said, looking at Cecily, expecting her to find all of this as ridiculous as she did. But for some reason, Cecily was just sitting there smiling obediently.

Since when does Cecily pop the Coco pills? Haley wondered.

"Before we start the lottery . . ." Coco began, opening the binder. Haley's eyes widened as she recognized headshots of fellow classmates, with notes in the margins in Coco and Whitney's handwriting.

"I think we should plan my table," Coco added, pulling out a seating chart.

"Where am I again?" Whitney asked, innocently.

"Here." Coco pointed to the place setting immediately to her left on the diagram. "You're next to Drew.

And I'm still not sure who's sitting here," she said slowly, eyeing Cecily and Haley as she pointed to the seat on her right.

"Shouldn't your sister sit there?" Haley proposed innocently.

Coco glared at her. "My sister is *not* sitting next to me." She penciled in Alison's name at the far end of the table. "She'll sit right next to my annoying aunt and uncle from Long Island."

"Why can't Cecily and Haley *both* sit at your table with us?" Whitney whined.

"Whitney, we've been over this already. My parents have invited friends and family. And since they are paying for the party, naturally there are certain *concessions* I have to make. Which means there is only one spot available for another girl at my table." She looked at Haley and Cecily. "The problem is, there are two of you," Coco purred.

"So what are you going to do?" Whitney asked, leaning back on the sofa.

"I haven't decided just yet," said Coco. She watched Haley's and Cecily's reactions closely, as if looking for clues, and added, "But I've got a pretty good idea. So, there. I'm thinking masquerade ball. Everyone wears masks until midnight."

"I love it!" Whitney said brightly.

"Of course you do, Whitney. That's why you're here." Coco patted her on the head.

"Sounds good to me," Cecily chimed in, once again going with the flow.

What is going on? Haley thought, wondering why Cecily was still kissing up to Coco. She decided it would be up to her to make any objections. "I think it's a little much, don't you? You won't recognize anyone."

"Duh," Whitney said. "That's sort of the point."

"No, but I mean, it won't be much fun if all those people are coming up to you, saying happy birthday, and you don't even know who they are. Right?" Haley said. "It's so close to Christmas, why don't you just go with a winter white theme?"

Coco's face contorted. "Because holiday balls are so obvious," she said.

"So obvious you didn't think of it yourself?" Cecily asked, before biting her lip.

"It's classic," said Haley. "There's a difference."

Whitney looked at Haley. "Well, my vote is still for Jungle Boogie. Everyone could wear animal print dresses and furs and there would be tropical flowers and exotic dancers and you could have, like, a white tiger in a cage."

"And you know where I stand on that idea. Moving on," said Coco.

"I still like your theme best, Coco," Cecily said robotically.

I liked you so much better when you had a spine, Haley thought.

"What do you say to cappuccinos after school?" Coco asked, postponing any final decisions about the theme until later in the day.

"I can't today," Cecily said, gathering up her books.

"Did I ask you?" Coco said, looking harshly at Cecily, who just shrugged off the snub. "What about you, Haley?"

"Umm," Haley said, stalling. She was baffled as to why Coco had suddenly taken such an interest in her. Especially since she'd done nothing but disagree with her for the past half hour.

"I guess," said Haley half-heartedly. "But I want to go to Bean Town. They have the only decaf latte I like. See ya." And with that, Haley breezed out of the library without waiting for Coco's response.

●　●　●

If you think Haley is turned off by Coco's manipulative tactics, have her GO HOME (page 237) and attempt to keep her distance from Ms. De Clerq. If you think Haley should get to know Coco on a deeper level—that is, if Coco De Clerq even has a deeper level—send her to COFFEE WITH COCO on page 231.

SASHA'S MOM ARRIVES

Frenchwomen don't get fat, they get even.

Sasha moved in with the Highlands until her mother could make arrangements to move to the U.S.

At first, she was bitter about the idea. She refused to talk about it whenever Haley came over to check up on her. But as the reunion approached, Sasha seemed to gradually warm to the prospect of being part of a family again.

Barbara Highland had been filling her in on all the details of her mothers life since she'd left Hillsdale—details that had all been recorded in letters sent to

Sasha through the years, letters that Sasha had never even bothered to open.

Finally, she was beginning to understand why her mother had left Hillsdale, and why, at the time, it had been impossible to take her daughter with her to Paris. What Sasha discovered was that Mrs. Lewis had gone back to school to finish her degree, so that someday she would be able to support the two of them on her own.

Sasha, meanwhile, had stopped drinking and was attending classes regularly with Reese and Haley. Most importantly, Luke Lawson was out of her life.

Once Luke's crash pad was no longer an option, he conveniently disappeared, and miraculously, the Hillsdale High thefts ceased, just like that.

Somehow, through it all, Sasha and Johnny's relationship had survived—which was why, even though everyone else at Hillsdale welcomed the old Sasha back into the fold, Coco De Clerq and Whitney Klein continued to freeze her out.

"I just don't understand," Sasha told Haley after school one day, while they were sitting in the Millers' basement. "Johnny's been good for me. He's been the one trying to keep me out of trouble. Why can't they see that?"

Haley reassured her. "You of all people should know that Coco and Whitney only see what they want to see."

Haley knew that Coco was planning an over-the-top sweet sixteen party, and just as she suspected, when it came time to hand out invitations, Reese got an invite, and so did Haley, but not Sasha, and certainly not Johnny Lane.

Luckily, the invitations arrived on the same day Sasha's mother was due in from Paris, so Sasha at least had something to distract her.

"Nervous?" Haley asked in the back of the limo on the way to the airport. Sasha nodded. "Don't be," said Haley. "She's your mom. And hello, you're Sasha Lewis. What's not to love?"

"She's right. You've got nothing to worry about, Sash," Reese said, squeezing her hand.

They arrived in front of the airport and scanned the faces of the people pouring out of the terminal. Finally, Reese spotted Sasha's mom. She was wearing a belted trench coat over a slim black dress and dark sunglasses. Even under all that, Haley could tell she was gorgeous.

Mrs. Lewis waved.

Sasha paused for a moment, then started walking, then running toward her mom.

"I love reunions," Haley said as Reese took her hand.

Later that night, after they'd all had dinner and Sasha's mom had gone upstairs to her room at the Highlands' to sleep off her jet lag, Reese, Haley, and Sasha sat around in Haley's basement. "I wish we could all go to Coco's party together," said Haley.

"Don't worry about it, Haley," Sasha said. "You and Reese should go. I'll hang out with Johnny. Besides, I want to introduce him to my mom. We figured meeting him on the same night she saw me for the first time in five years might be a little much."

"There's no way we're ditching you for Coco," said Reese.

"Thanks," said Sasha. "But you really don't have to."

Haley smiled mischievously. "I've got an idea," she said. "Why don't we crash it?"

"What do you mean, just show up?" Sasha said.

"Sure, why not. The invitation says it's a costume party. No one will ever know the difference," said Haley.

"We are members of the country club," Reese offered. "Technically, they can't keep us out."

"Speak for yourself," said Sasha. "My father let our membership lapse ages ago."

"Come on, Sash," Haley said. "You've got to stand up to her. You can't give in and expect her to stop treating you like this."

"It's just," Sasha said, "as rude as she's been, she is one of my oldest friends. I don't want to spoil her party."

"How could *you* spoil anyone's party?" Reese asked, wrapping his arm around her.

"Believe me, it's possible," said Sasha. "A few weeks ago, I got loaded at Richie Huber's and threw up in the punch bowl."

"How about this?" said Haley. "We flip a coin.

Heads we all crash, Johnny included. Tails we all skip it."

"Does tails mean I get to have some peace and quiet with Johnny and my mom?" Sasha asked.

"Sure," said Reese. "Haley and I will just have to figure out something to do on our own."

"Sounds good to me," said Haley. She took a quarter out of her pocket, tossed it in the air and held her breath to see which side it would land on.

● ● ●

If you want it to be heads, turn to CRASH COCO'S SWEET SIXTEEN (page 246). If you want it to be tails, turn to DATE WITH REESE (page 241). Alternatively, if you think Coco should be punished for being so cruel to Sasha, turn to SABOTAGE COCO'S SWEET SIXTEEN (page 213).

TURN HER IN

If someone looks guilty and acts guilty, they usually are guilty.

Seeing Sasha walk into a known drug dealer's house wasn't something Haley was equipped to deal with. When another car arrived and two thugs got out and went inside, Haley told the cabbie to drive her straight to the police station. She spilled her guts to the first cop who crossed her path.

Not only was Sasha picked up at the drug den and charged with possession and "intent to distribute," but Hillsdale's finest also figured out that Sasha Lewis was presently without a legal guardian.

Sasha ended up spending the next three months

in a juvenile detention center, and another three months in foster care. That was precisely how long it took her mother to move to the U.S., establish legal residency and hire a lawyer to get custody back.

Unfortunately, all that time in juvie and shuffling around foster homes took its toll on Sasha. She came back to Hillsdale six months later with a dozen body piercings and her hair dyed jet black.

Haley was never able to get over the guilt she felt for turning in her friend and was plagued by the thought that if only she'd gone to her parents first, Sasha's life would've somehow been different.

● ● ●

Go back to page 1.

STUBBLE TROUBLE

Hot and bothered isn't always a good thing.

After Haley's marathon makeout session with Sebastian, her sensitive skin was raw from rubbing up against his five o'clock shadow. By the next morning, blisters had formed on her chin.

Haley's parents quickly figured out what she'd been up to, and unfortunately, so did everyone at school the following week.

Haley Miller's nickname for the rest of the school year? Spanish Rug Burn.

Hang your head and go back to page 1.

PATCHWORK

Even in a great relationship, you can sometimes see the seams.

Haley tracked down Dave in the library at school the following Monday. "So is it true you're going to Coco's sixteenth birthday instead of Annie's?" she demanded.

"Shhhh!" he whispered, pointing to the other students studying.

"Well?" Haley said, waiting for an answer.

"It's not that simple," said Dave, escorting her to a study room.

"Why not?" Haley asked, once they were alone. "She's your girlfriend, isn't she?"

Dave sighed. "Hannah asked me if I'd help with the Rubber Dynamite show. I didn't know it was Annie's birthday."

"So cancel," said Haley.

"I gave Hannah my word," Dave said.

"So you're missing Annie's birthday to go to the party of a spoiled, manipulative brat who's spent the last seven years torturing her? Awesome. Did you know Coco has been purposely ruining Annie's birthday ever since the third grade?"

"Gosh, when you put it that way . . ." Dave sighed.

"And this year, thanks to you, Coco's done it once again."

"Poor Annie," said Dave. "She must be so upset."

"Of course she's upset," Haley said, not about to let him off the hook. "She thinks you've deserted her for Coco, or worse, Hannah Moss."

"Hannah and I are just friends."

"You know that, and I know that. But does Annie know that?"

"So what do I do?" Dave asked.

"Well, first you need to explain the situation to Hannah. Ask her to find someone else to help her with Coco's party. And then you need to order flowers. And send them to her, Annie, preferably in a public place. Then, after you take Annie to dinner and apologize, you need to help me start planning the ultimate surprise party for her. Try to think of people who'd rather celebrate with Annie than Coco.

There must be *someone* at school Coco De Clerq hasn't gotten to yet."

At that moment, Haley spotted Coco, Whitney and Cecily huddled together on a sofa in an alcove near the fire escape. They were giggling and looking through the pages of a big blue binder in Coco's lap.

They're up to something, Haley thought. *Probably trying to destroy someone else's life.*

"Well, what are you waiting for?" Haley said to Dave. "Get moving!"

Dave collected his things and scrambled out of the library.

Haley, meanwhile, still had some research to do. A little research that involved figuring out how to pay Coco back.

● ● ●

To get even with Coco for spoiling Annie's birthday for all those years, turn to SABOTAGE COCO'S SWEET SIXTEEN (page 213). To throw Annie a party she'll never forget, turn to SURPRISE ANNIE on page 252.

There are two ways of making amends. Taking the high road. Or crawling down into the gutter.

SABOTAGE COCO'S SWEET SIXTEEN

Living well isn't the best revenge. Getting even is.

Haley had officially had it with Coco De Clerq. She was tired of the spitefulness, the manipulation, the petty, mean-spirited mind games. Coco's evil empire was founded on hurting people Haley cared about, and it was time to put a stop to it, once and for all.

In just the three or so months Haley had been at Hillsdale, Coco had turned one of the coolest, nicest girls at school, Cecily Watson, into another one of her clones.

And then there was Sasha Lewis. The former BFF of Coco and Whitney had been dumped by her two best friends at one of roughest moments of her life.

But the worst, by far, of Coco's offenses was ruining Annie Armstrong's birthday for seven years straight.

Someone needs to give this girl a taste of her own medicine, Haley decided. *And since no one else in Hillsdale is volunteering for the job, it's up to me to do it.*

In the final week leading up to Coco's sweet sixteen party, Haley began plotting the most efficient way to sabotage the jungle boogie–themed event. Detail by meticulous detail, Haley devised ways to undo all of Coco and Whitney's hard work. *Seven acts of sabotage,* Haley thought, *one for each of the seven years Coco wrecked Annie Armstrong's birthday.*

Day one: Haley found Whitney's annotated yearbook in the trash in front of the Kleins' house. This was the copy that Coco and Whitney had cut up for their infamous loser lottery. From it, Haley compiled a list of the people Coco had deemed too "undesirable" to invite to her party. Once their home addresses were added, Haley took the list to a fancy stationery store in town, where she knew Coco was having her invitations printed up. Haley gave it to the woman behind the counter and told her that Coco De Clerq had asked her to drop off the final guest list for the party.

Day two: Haley broke into Coco's gym locker and added olive oil and cocoa butter to her bottle of "oil-free" face lotion. *That should help clear up her complexion,* Haley thought.

Day three: Haley staked out the hair salon Coco had used religiously since the sixth grade—low lights every six weeks and a monthly overall gloss—located Coco's color card and changed all the numbers on her chart to correspond with bright red and orange dyes on the color wheel.

Perfect, Haley calculated. *Coco's next appointment is the day of her party.*

Day four: Haley hacked into Coco's school e-mail account and sent a message to the florist at the country club, saying that she had impulsively changed her mind about the entire jungle boogie theme. Now, instead of the tropical island flowers, she wanted dyed blue and gold carnations mixed with sprays of white baby's breath. "You know, for the Hillsdale High School colors," she typed.

Day five: Haley called the caterer, pretending to be Coco. "My parents have cut my budget in half," she said, breaking down hysterically. "I am so sorry about the last-minute notice, you guys, but instead of the surf and turf, we need pigs in blankets and spray cheese."

Day six: Haley called Rubber Dynamite and cancelled their performance. Then she called a local party planning agency and ordered a Karaoke machine and a dancing clown, insisting that he or she be capable of making balloon animals of all shapes and sizes.

Day seven: Since Coco had arranged for two white tigers to perform onstage as the grand finale of her party, Haley called the animal trainer and made sure the tigers were replaced with two Vietnamese potbellied pigs.

A brilliant plan, if I do say so myself, Haley thought, after borrowing one of her father's digital video cameras. She spent the night of Coco's party documenting the whole disastrous affair, and then made copies, offering them for free to every person Coco had ever hurt, offended or snubbed.

THE END

CONFRONT COCO

Even if the truth doesn't set you free, it sure feels good to say it.

Ugh! *Just look at the way she walks!* Haley thought, watching Coco do her "meet and greets" in the hallway. *Who does she think she is?*

"What's up, Haley?" Coco said breezily as they crossed paths.

"Your nose," Haley replied. "It's pointed straight in the air."

Coco stopped in her tracks. "What did you say?"

"You heard me," Haley said, looking at Coco. "You're stuck up. You're a total brat, and everyone knows it. It's creepy, the way you lord it over everyone at this school, just assuming that we all care who you are."

"Noted and filed under opinions of me that don't matter," Coco said sternly.

"I'm not done with you yet," said Haley.

"You should be careful, Miller. You're still relatively new here, so a certain amount of . . . impertinence . . . can be forgiven. But with each day that passes, you seal your fate just a little bit more by hanging out with people like Annie Armstrong. Your chances of being anything other than a wannabe like her are slipping farther and farther away."

"Am I supposed to be scared by that threat, Coco? Keep quiet and play nice, Haley, and maybe I'll let you sit with me in the cafeteria? No thanks. I'd rather not share a table with No Eat and Repeat."

Coco's eyes widened. "So, you've been talking to Annie about me, have you?"

"Yep, and Annie also told me what you did to her. What kind of person ruins someone's birthday for seven years straight?"

"You should never pass judgment without hearing both sides," said Coco.

"Please. There is absolutely nothing you could say that could possibly justify what you've done."

"It's not my fault that Annie can't get over the past. In her mind, this is all still about her. Trust me, Haley. Annie is just one of those people who always thinks the world has wronged them. And right now, the villain just happens to be me."

"So you think this is all in Annie's head?"

"Listen, come to my party," Coco suggested. "I can promise you'll have a good time, and quite frankly, you could use a different perspective on life in Hillsdale right now. If it makes you feel any better, we can call Annie up right now and invite her to come too."

What's she up to? Haley wondered.

"But it has to be on my terms," Coco said, folding her arms across her chest.

● ● ●

If you think Haley should believe Coco and accept the invitation, send Haley to COCO'S SWEET SIXTEEN (page 262). If that head game made you want to test Annie Armstrong's loyalty, go to page 258 and TEST ANNIE. You can send Haley to SABOTAGE COCO'S SWEET SIXTEEN on page 213 if you think Coco needs to be taught a lesson. And finally, you can ignore Coco altogether and turn to page 252 to SURPRISE ANNIE for her birthday.

WORLDS COLLIDE

If you like two friends equally, it doesn't necessarily follow that they'll like each other.

Haley and Gretchen woke up early on Saturday and drank decaf coffee and fresh orange juice while reading the *San Francisco Chronicle* on the Wallers' stone terrace. It was just the way they used to spend weekend mornings after sleepovers, before Haley had moved East. She was relieved that Gretchen was finally starting to seem like her old self again.

Since Mrs. Waller worked most Saturdays and had already headed to the office for the day, and Mr. Waller was at the golf course, Haley wondered how they were going to get around. "Which bus route should we take to the museum?" she asked.

"Bus?" said Gretchen. "We don't need to take the bus. I'm driving."

"What?" asked Haley, stunned. "Your parents bought you a car?"

"My mom's so busy these days, how do you think I get to and from school and all my acting lessons?"

Haley couldn't believe it. "Do you know the driving age is seventeen in New Jersey?" she said.

"Ouch. Yet another reason to hate the state."

"Hey," said Haley. "You're talking about my people."

"Yeah, you so totally strike me as a Jersey girl," said Gretchen. "I just can't wait to meet the leather jackets and gelled hair."

"They're not like that," said Haley. "You'll see."

After they had finished their breakfast, Haley put on her favorite jeans, a blue vintage T-shirt and the low-top sneakers she and Gretchen had purposely mismatched before the Millers moved to New Jersey.

Gretchen, meanwhile, wore a slim black boat neck top and skirt with flat black sandals and her signature black oversized sunglasses.

"I probably should've brought some nicer clothes," Haley said self-consciously, looking at Gretchen's outfit.

"Do you want to borrow something?" Gretchen offered.

"That's okay," said Haley. She could only imagine what Irene, Shaun and Devon would say if they both showed up looking like Audrey Hepburn clones.

"I can't believe you're still wearing those sneakers!" Gretchen said when she saw Haley's shoes. "My mom made me throw mine out when I wore through one of the soles."

"You threw away our sneakers?" said Haley, shocked.

"Well, actually, I only told my mom I threw them out. They're still in my closet," Gretchen added with a mischievous look. "Whatever you do, keep Judy Waller away from door number three."

Haley followed Gretchen to the garage, where an expensive-looking black sedan was waiting for them.

"*This* is your car?" said Haley.

"I know, it's a little extravagant, but my dad says it's got one of the best safety records on the road," said Gretchen as they got into the pristine car and buckled up. "My parents feel better knowing I'm riding around the city in this instead of some little tin can."

"Double wow. If I'd known we had wheels, I would've told Irene and the boys we'd pick them up at the hotel. There's even enough room in here for Shaun," said Haley.

"We can call them now if you like," Gretchen offered, picking up her cell phone.

"That's okay," said Haley. "They're probably

already on their way. Besides, I like us hanging out again."

"Just like old times," said Gretchen, repeating their refrain for the weekend. She backed out onto the Wallers' stone driveway and past the ornate shrubbery edging their property.

"Yep, just like old times," Haley said, although she was thinking, *Only now you look like a movie star, live in a mansion and drive a car that's nicer than my parents' brand-new hybrid SUV.*

Irene, Shaun and Devon were waiting for them in front of the museum, looking not unlike the Three Stooges.

"Well, I guess you don't have to point out Shaun," Gretchen said, eyeing him from a distance. Shaun, of course, was Curly. "Tell me again how *he* arranged for a private tour of the MOMA?"

"Shaun's parents are big donors," said Haley. "They're in town for some meeting about a new acquisition."

"Interesting," said Gretchen.

"Time's a-wasting, hoss," Shaun greeted them as Haley and Gretchen approached.

"Everyone, this is Gretchen. Gretchen, Shaun, Devon, Irene."

"It's a pleasure. Haley's told me so much about you," Gretchen said diplomatically.

"Haley talks about you all the time too," said Devon.

"We were in diapers together," said Haley.

"Nappy mates, I get it," said Shaun.

"You're practically twins," Irene added sarcastically, looking at Haley's worn jeans and T-shirt and Gretchen's perfect, slimming ensemble.

Devon leaned over and kissed Haley on the cheek, wrapping his arm around her waist.

Gretchen watched the two of them with interest. The look on her face said, *Why didn't you tell me you had a boyfriend?* "I'm so glad to know Haley's made such good friends on the East Coast," she said. "We were worried about her when she moved."

"Whatever," said Irene. "Let's just go inside. I don't want to be late."

Why is she being so rude? Haley wondered. She almost felt the need to apologize to Gretchen. Then Haley remembered she had only herself to blame. After all, she was the one who had complained to Irene about Gretchen's behavior the previous night. Now, it seemed, Gretchen was fair game. Haley suddenly realized that getting all her friends to like one another was going to be a lot harder than she had originally thought.

"Dude, I think I'm in love," Shaun said two hours later as they emerged from the museum. He leaned against Haley, batting his eyelashes.

"With whom?" Haley asked, casually tossing aside Shaun's burly arm.

"Robert Rauschenberg," said Shaun. "And Gerhard Richter. And de Kooning."

"My heart belongs to Tina Barney," said Devon, "and Cindy Sherman, and maybe Lee Friedlander."

"I loved that Max Beckmann," said Gretchen. "And the little Elizabeth Peyton? So sweet."

"Liam and Noel," Haley said, remembering the painting that depicted the Gallagher brothers from the band Oasis. "Did you ever think you'd see a picture of the guys who sang 'Wonderwall' hanging in a museum?"

"Are you an Oasis fan, Gretchen?" Irene asked, her voice tinged with sarcasm.

Uh-oh, Haley thought.

Shaun began singing. "I said maybe, maybe, maybe . . . you're gonna be the one that saves me, that saves me, that saves me . . . ," he belted out, providing his own studio echo.

"No, actually," said Gretchen. "I'm not an especially big Oasis fan. If you ask me, they're just another Manchester nostalgia band with bad haircuts."

Here it comes, Haley thought, ducking for cover in Shaun's embrace, *that famous Waller temper.*

"But I do like modern portraiture," Gretchen continued. She wasn't about to let Irene Chen make her look stupid for liking a painting of two rocker dudes. "You know, Lucian Freud, Alice Neel, some of the sixties- and seventies-era David Hockneys."

Ouch, Haley thought. *Integration not going well. Abort mission! Abort mission!* Irene didn't respond. Haley finally said, hoping to take things down a notch, "Anyone hungry?"

They all silently piled into Gretchen's car and headed toward Chinatown, where they were supposed to meet Irene's great-aunt for lunch.

Maybe this will put her more at ease, Haley thought hopefully.

After a brief stop at the Chinese railroad workers mural, they arrived at the address Great-aunt Mimi Chen had given Irene. But when they got there, they found no restaurant and no sign for anything known as the Jade Lily.

Just as they were about to give up and head down to the waterfront, an alley door opened and an older Asian woman dressed in a beige silk top, black pants and slippers emerged.

"This way," she said without bothering to stop for introductions. They all looked at one another, confused. Haley shrugged and followed the woman through the door, up a narrow staircase, past several apartment doors and into a large living room that was outfitted with a dozen or so small tables and chairs. The place was packed with Asian immigrants, most of them chattering in Chinese or Korean.

"This, Jade Lily," the woman, who Haley figured was Aunt Mimi, said. "Come, sit."

They followed her, enticed by the delicious smells coming out of the kitchen, to a table in the back, where they all sat down.

"What is this place?" Gretchen asked.

"I guess it's some sort of underground restaurant," Haley whispered.

"We eat now," said Aunt Mimi. And just like that, bowls of steaming hot soup dumplings arrived at their table. They all followed Mimi's lead, picking up their spoons and chopsticks to dig into the warm, tangy morsels filled with sweet-and-sour pork and broth. The dumplings were strange, certainly unlike anything Haley had ever tasted at the Golden Dynasty back home, but delicious.

Next came the pork buns. Then a dish of garlicky broccoli shoots. When the shark soup arrived, Shaun looked like he might pass out from sheer pleasure. Each dish was such an explosion of new tastes and smells, Haley wondered how she'd ever be able to eat regular old sweet and sour chicken again.

After lunch, once they'd thanked Aunt Mimi and said their goodbyes, Haley and the others went in search of the car.

"Papa got a brand-new chin," Shaun blurted out, holding his belly. "Them pork buns almost top the banana sandwich, hoss. Definitely worth busting a gut."

"I wish my parents would open a restaurant like that," Irene said, deep in thought.

"So convince them to do it," Haley said. "Aren't they planning to open a new branch next spring? Why don't you see if they'll try using a more authentic menu."

"Are you kidding?" said Irene. "If it's not fried and doused in a sugary sauce, it doesn't land on a Golden Dynasty plate."

"You'll never know unless you try," Gretchen said supportively.

"So what's next, kids?" Haley asked.

Irene, Shaun and Devon shrugged, almost in unison. *Yep, the Three Stooges,* Haley thought.

"I've got an idea," said Gretchen as they reached the car.

"What's that?" Irene asked skeptically.

"Trust me," said Gretchen. They all piled into the sedan, and a few minutes later they arrived at Pier 45. Gretchen parked and said, "Here we are, kids, the Musée Mécanique."

"Radical," said Devon, jumping out of the car and looking into the hall of antique arcade games.

"Thanks," Haley said, smiling at Gretchen. "This is *perfect.*"

Once inside, Shaun dragged them all over to a towering, redheaded clown named Laffing Sal. The doll had a terrifying face that was repelling small children, but Shaun seemed smitten. "Oh, yeah," he said, pressing his body up against the glass.

Devon took out his camera and snapped a photo of Shaun pretending to kiss the maniacally laughing Sal.

"Laffing Sal, here, and her partner, Laffing Sam, were a part of almost every fun house in the United States during the thirties and forties," Irene said, summarizing the fact sheet she'd picked up at the entrance. "So I guess that makes you Laffing Shaun."

"Now, that's a Bizarre Love Triangle," said Haley.

"Check this out." Gretchen grabbed Irene's arm and walked her over to a mechanical diorama of a circus. She popped in twenty-five cents, bringing the tiny carnival to life inside the glass cabinet. Irene, in spite of herself, marveled at the thouands of tiny moving parts. She turned to Gretchen and said, "Cool."

Watching her two very different best friends stand there together, Haley suddenly realized, she and her friends would always change, either growing toward each other or growing apart. The important thing was to find ways to reconnect.

Haley wandered toward the back of the museum and found her favorite old gypsy wishing machine, the one her parents had given her countless quarters for through the years. She slipped yet another coin into the slot, watching the old bearded fortune-teller come to life. Haley closed her eyes and made a wish. As the fortune-teller froze once again, a yellow ticket appeared.

She bent over, picked it up, and read it. *Your wish has been granted.*

Haley looked around, and sure enough, there was Devon examining an old black-and-white photo booth not far from where she was standing.

"Let's take some pictures," Haley said, tugging him by the hand. They climbed into the booth and pulled the velvet curtain closed behind them, making goofy faces in front of the lens.

Just as the last shot was about to flash, Devon

turned to Haley. "Ever since I met you, I've been wanting to do this," he said, as he leaned in and kissed her gently on the lips.

Miraculously, their perfect moment had been captured on film. Looking at the photo strip as it dried, Haley suddenly realized why her father was a filmmaker, and why Devon loved taking pictures. She had the sudden urge to go home and dig up the old Super 8 her father had given her for her thirteenth birthday.

"What is it?" Devon asked.

"Nothing," said Haley, with a faraway look in her eye. "It's just that I think I just got my wish."

Devon kissed her again, but what he didn't know, what he couldn't have known, was that Haley hadn't wished for him.

She had asked the old gypsy to find her true passion in life. And she was beginning to think that was just what the old bearded man had done.

THE END

Who needs artificial stimulants when you've got a steady dose of Coco De Clerq?

"I'll have a small decaf skinny cap," Coco ordered. "And you better make sure to use nonfat milk."

"And for you, miss?" the Bean Town cashier asked Haley.

"A decaf latte, please. Whole milk," she said, emphasis on the *whole,* even though Coco clearly disapproved of the order.

"What's your name?" the cashier asked, armed with a black marker, ready to mark the coffee cups.

"Susan Simmons," Coco answered matter-of-factly.

What's she up to now? Haley wondered, for the moment playing along.

"What's with the alias?" Haley asked, once they'd found a table."

"Just watch," Coco replied, motioning toward the barista.

"Thuthan Thimmonth?" the barista called out in a heavy, hilarious lisp. "Thuthan. Thuthan Thimmonth?" He was holding up the two coffee cups, and seemed oblivious to his own speech impediment. Haley started to go retrieve their coffee, but Coco stopped her.

"Not yet," Coco said, holding out her arm.

The barista called out a third time, "Ith there a Thuthan Thimmonth in the houth?"

"Can I go now?" Haley asked.

"Fine, but you're no fun," said Coco.

Haley collected their cups.

Back at the table, Coco took the lid off her coffee and stirred in an artificial sweetener, while Haley sprinkled two packets of raw sugar into hers.

"So, why do you think you should be seated at the De Clerq family table?" Coco asked.

"I don't," Haley said matter-of-factly. "I wouldn't presume to expect a seat at the head table. We haven't known each other that long. And I think Cecily wants it more than I do, anyway."

Coco was baffled. Clearly no one had ever treated one of her invitations with so little regard before.

"This is why I told Matt Graham he shouldn't go for you," said Coco. "You're not hungry enough."

As opposed to you, who's hungry all the time, Haley thought, looking at Coco's protruding collarbone. "When were you talking to Matt Graham about me?" she asked.

"He's sort of gotten it into his head that he has a crush on you." Coco smiled. "But don't worry. I told Matt you couldn't possibly like him, since you're still stuck on Reese Highland."

Haley wasn't sure how that news made her feel. It wasn't Coco's place to be manipulating her love life. But then again, Coco did have a point. Was Matt really a guy Haley could like? Or was she doomed to compare every other boy at Hillsdale to Reese Highland?

"I know what you're thinking," Coco said. "He's not quite as tall as Reese. Or as good-looking. But he's way into you, and I'm beginning to think Reese may not be capable of that. If you know what I mean."

Haley rolled her eyes. "Just because Reese doesn't like you, doesn't mean he's not into girls, Coco. He's just . . . saving himself. And I respect that."

"Oh, please, honey," said Coco. "The only thing boys our age want saving from is abstinence. He could have any girl he wanted and yet he doesn't. So what does that say, huh?"

"I don't know," Haley admitted.

"Now, on to the real reason why we're here. The guest list," said Coco. "One person we know we won't be inviting—Annie Armstrong. You know, the brownnoser in our Spanish class?"

"Yeah, sure," Haley said. "I know Annie. Our moms work together. She doesn't seem that bad to me."

"She ruined my birthday in third grade, and it's my personal mission in life to make sure she never lives it down."

"Really?"

"I can't believe I've never told you this story," Coco said.

"What happened?" Haley asked.

Coco paused, looked around, leaned toward her and whispered, "The girl peed on me."

"She *peed* on you?" Haley repeated in disbelief. "What do you mean she *peed* on you?"

"Keep it down," Coco chided. "Annie and I have the same birthday. We used to have a joint party. Well, really, I just used to let Annie come to my parties and pretend they were hers too. When we turned nine, I had twenty of my best friends sleeping over that night."

Only Coco would have twenty best friends in the third grade, Haley thought.

"At some point, I banished Annie to the couch in the den because she was being, well, Annie. And then in the middle of the night, after we had all finally fallen asleep, she came into my room, got into

234

my bed with me and peed all over me. On my new Egyptian cotton bedding. Which my parents had given me special for the occasion. It was the most disgusting thing ever. I had to take like twelve showers and have my entire room redecorated. Needless to say, we burned the sheets."

"But you don't think she did it on purpose?" Haley said. "She was probably just sleepwalking."

"Oh no," said Coco. "I'm sure she knew what she was doing. Would you believe she even tried to blame it on my dog? Not even a dog would do something that gross, and certainly not my Clemmy."

"You must have been furious."

"Oh, I didn't get mad," Coco said matter-of-factly. "I got even. Every year since, I've had the biggest, most outrageous birthday party my parents would pay for."

"And let me guess, you've never invited Annie."

"Nope. I just invite all her closest friends, who sell her out and come to my parties instead. Funny how that works. Nowadays, it seems like she doesn't even have any friends."

Haley had never heard of anyone holding a grudge for seven years. Even if Annie had peed on Coco, the punishment seemed to far outweigh the crime. "Don't you think it's time you forgive and forget?" Haley suggested. "Why not invite Annie this year? What could it hurt?"

"Um, like everything," said Coco. "Hello, it's Annie Armstrong. She'll ruin everything. Besides, my sweet sixteen is going to be the best. Birthday. Ever! There's no way I'm going to let a loser like Annie spoil the fun."

● ● ●

This is it. To send send Haley to COCO'S SWEET SIX-TEEN, turn to page 262. If you think Haley feels bad for Annie Armstrong after hearing how Coco has been pun-ishing her all these years, have Haley SURPRISE ANNIE with a party on page 252. If you think Coco is the one who deserves the payback, turn to SABOTAGE COCO'S SWEET SIXTEEN on page 213.

**Anyone can get caught.
It just takes the right
kind of bait.**

Haley plopped down in front of her computer, hoping for a chat with one of her friends from California. Instead, an instant message from Coco popped up.

    C: We need to talk.

Haley debated whether or not to write her back.

    H: What's up?
    C: Cecily Watson's been trash
       talking you all over school. I

just thought you'd want to
know.

Haley frowned. *That doesn't seem like something
Cecily would do.*

H: I find that a little hard to
   believe. What did she say?
C: Well, for starters, she told
   our entire table at lunch
   today that you've been
   stalking Reese Highland.

Haley's mouth dropped.

H: That's crazy!
C: I know. But she said Reese has
   been calling her to complain
   about you.
H: Nice try, Coco. But I don't
   believe you.
C: She told everyone how you've
   been spying on him from your
   window. And have you, I don't
   know, stopped by his house
   unannounced recently?
H: My mother sent me next door
   with a basket of muffins
   yesterday. But Reese wasn't
   even there!

C: And did you leave a message
   for him?
H: Yeah. I told his mom to say
   hi.
C: You didn't! He sort of took
   that as a hint.
H: Hint about what?
C: That you're obsessed with him.
   That you want to marry him and
   have his babies.
H: That's ridiculous.
C: You know how boys are. They
   have to be the ones to make
   the first move.
H: I'm calling Reese right now to
   clear things up. He can't
   possibly think that about me.
C: I wouldn't do that if I were
   you, Haley. He'll just think
   you're, well, stalking him
   again.
H: I'm signing off now.
C: Don't you want to know what
   else Cecily said? Think back to
   that embarrassing little secret
   you confided in her recently.

Haley mentally sifted through every conversation
she and Cecily had shared recently, about chemistry
homework, directions to get through the math wing,

what they were each planning to wear to Coco's upcoming Sweet Sixteen party, and . . . *Oh, no,* Haley thought.

```
H: She didn't. Cecily wouldn't
   dare.
C: Oh, honey. She so did.
```

● ● ●

If you think Haley should vent about Cecily over IM, TAKE THE BAIT on page 268. If you think Haley really likes Cecily for who she is and believe that Coco is just up to her manipulative tricks again, turn to page 271, STAY TRUE.

Isn't it convenient when what you want is right next door?

At 7:02, Reese Highland rang the doorbell at the Miller residence.

"I've got it!" Haley called out. "Bye, Mom! Bye, Dad! See ya, Mitchell!" she said, trying to slip down the stairs and out the front door before her parents could sit Reese down for a chat.

"Where are you kids going for dinner?" Joan asked from the kitchen.

"Somewhere close," Haley said. "I'll be home by curfew."

"Have fun," Joan called out.

Have fun? What is going on? Haley wondered. *Since when do Joan and Perry let me out of the house on a date without okaying my outfit, checking the battery life on my cell phone and grilling the boy for twenty minutes about our planned itinerary?* Then she suddenly realized, *Since the boy is Reese Highland.*

Haley had finally settled on wearing a blue A-line coat, a white blouse, a navy skirt and brown boots. She adjusted her skirt, reapplied her lip gloss one last time, and opened the door.

Reese was standing on the front porch in his brown barn jacket and scarf, smiling. "Hi," he said. "You look great."

"I didn't know where we were going, so I wasn't sure how to dress," Haley admitted. "That's why I love navy. It's a pretty universal color." *Stop babbling!* Haley told herself. *It's only Reese. Pretend like you're in the basement playing video games.*

"How does Italian food sound?" he asked as they walked down the driveway toward the green and white taxicab that was waiting for them at the curb.

"Wow, chariot service? I could've worn heels. I mean, Italian sounds perfect," she said, climbing into the backseat next to Reese.

Reese gave directions to the cabdriver and then returned his full attention to Haley. "I can't wait to see you on the field next soccer season," he said. "You're going to blow everyone away. I can just feel it."

"It's already torture not being able to run all the time."

"They're called Jimmy legs," Reese said.

"You get them too?" Haley asked, remembering the all-too-familiar feeling of tension in her hamstrings, quads and calves. "I don't know how I'm going to survive this winter!"

"Don't worry. Practice will start up again in the spring. Until then, we should start running together on the weekends. There are some great trails in our neighborhood. You just pile on the layers when it snows."

"Anything to get rid of the, what did you call them? Jimmy legs," Haley said. "I'll give you Jimmy legs," Reese said, squeezing her knee at a pressure point so it tickled.

"Hey!" Haley said. Just because I don't have my cleats on doesn't mean I can't kick you in the shins."

"Ref!" Reese called out to the cabbie.

After a fifteen-minute drive to the Hudson River's edge, the taxi pulled over at a quaint little colonial building with white Christmas lights decorating the shrubbery out front. The carved and painted wooden sign read SICILIAN SUN.

"Let's walk out on the pier for a minute first to check out the view," Reese suggested after he had paid the cabbie. "Here, take this," he said, and wrapped his scarf around Haley's neck, tying it gently beneath her chin.

As Haley and Reese walked out onto the pier together under the full moon, Reese took Haley's hand in his. The view of the distant lights of New York City and the luster of reflections in the water were magical. An occasional gust of wind made Haley snuggle closer to Reese, but otherwise, she was impressed by how utterly quiet and peaceful it was.

It's perfect, Haley thought, realizing it was the first moment since she and Reese had known each other when they had been completely alone, as in, not in the Millers' basement, with no friends or parents lurking nearby.

She looked up at him and smiled. "If I forget to tell you on the ride home, I had a really great time tonight," she said.

Reese was about to say something. He bit his lip and looked out at the water. And then suddenly, he kissed her. It was almost enough to make Haley forget that her toes and fingers were beginning to go numb from the cold.

"We should probably get you inside," Reese said when he felt her shivering. He took Haley's chilly hands in his and then wrapped his arms around her to warm her up.

"What's the opposite of Jimmy legs?" she asked, leaning against him, her knees quivering from the cold.

"My little California girl's got flamingo legs,"

Reese said, pulling her close and kissing her forehead. "Let's get you some pasta to warm you up."

Looking up at Reese, Haley realized there was a lot more than a big plate of pasta to look forward to.

THE END

CRASH COCO'S
SWEET SIXTEEN

There was nothing Joan Miller loved more than subverting the established order.

And since Coco and her ritzy themed birthday parties were definitely the established social order at Hillsdale High, Joan drove Haley and her friends to the costume shop and loaned them her credit card so that they could crash Coco's party and get her back for snubbing Sasha and all the other "undesirables" in their grade.

On the night of the party, Sasha, Johnny, Reese and Haley stood outside the Bergen Country

Club gates, dressed as seventeenth-century courtiers.

"Last chance to back out," said Johnny, who wasn't exactly psyched about wearing a powdered wig, short breeches and a mask. Haley was impressed he was there, though, especially since the Hedon's rival band, Rubber Dynamite, had been hired to play at the party.

"Johnny's right. This was a bad idea," said Sasha. "Haley, you and Reese stay and go to the party."

"You're staying," said Haley, tugging at her long brocade dress. "We didn't come all this way so that you could chicken out."

"What if someone recognizes us?" Sasha asked.

"Not a chance," Haley said, reassuring her. "*I* don't even recognize us. And I picked out the costumes."

"These knickers are too tight," Reese said, squirming.

"They'll loosen up once you start dancing," Haley assured him.

"You don't expect me to dance in this getup, do you?" Johnny whispered to Sasha. "Not to Rubber Dynamite."

"No," she said, giving him a peck on the lips. "It's enough that you came."

"Well, shall we crash?" said Reese.

"We shall," said Haley taking his arm. They walked up the long drive to the clubhouse, where, judging from the commotion and all the camera flashes, Coco De Clerq had just made her entrance.

"Hi there," an unidentifiable girl in a low-cut corset said to Reese as she waltzed into the party. Haley tightened her grip on his arm. They breezed past security without having to flash invitations.

"Told you," Haley said to Sasha. "That's the beauty of having great costumes. No one questions you."

"This is too funny," Sasha whispered, motioning to a girl teetering past them in high heels and a bustled getup with a long train that cut away to a miniskirt in front.

"You can't disguise that walk," Haley whispered back.

Sasha and Haley looked at each other and in unison said, "Whitney Klein."

The ballroom had been transformed, with red roses bursting from vases on the tables, gold velvet curtains draping the walls and thousands of candles casting the room in a perfect, warm, muted light.

Haley linked hands with Reese, afraid to lose him in the crowd. They followed Sasha and Johnny toward one of the bars, ordering a round of sparkling water for the four of them before parking themselves at a table.

"Look, there's Coco," Haley said, spotting the birthday princess prancing around the ballroom like a peacock. She was wearing a floor-length turquoise and gold satin gown, with a black feathered mask held up to her face.

"Are you sure she's not going to recognize us?"

Sasha asked, turning her back to her as Coco passed their table without so much as a glance.

Whitney ran up to Coco, her hands fluttering, and Haley momentarily thought they were caught, but she was only rushing over to Coco to compliment her dress.

"You look . . . ah-mazing," Whitney said.

"Ugh," Coco whined. "This dress weighs fifty pounds, and I absolutely *hate* this theme. I don't recognize anyone. And I don't have anyone to talk to."

"You have me," Whitney said brightly.

"Go get me a drink," Coco commanded. "I'm going to go check my messages again to see if Reese called."

As Coco stormed off, Reese slunk down in his chair, hiding behind Haley.

Haley turned to Sasha. "Why don't you go say something to her," she suggested gently.

"Like what? 'Surprise!' "

"Well, you could start with 'Happy birthday,' " Haley said. "Sasha, you care about her. Otherwise, we wouldn't be here tonight. So you owe it to yourself, and to the friendship, to try and patch things up."

"I know you're right," Sasha said finally, steeling herself for what she had to do. "Thanks," she said, giving Haley a hug and squeezing Johnny's hand before she wandered off in search of Coco.

"We'll be right here waiting," Haley said, leaning her head against Reese's shoulder.

"Dude, man. Coco De Clerq is obsessed with

you," Johnny said to Reese, while playing a drum solo on the table with two drink stirrers.

"Dude, don't remind me. It's been like this for a year. I keep hoping she'll get the message and leave me alone."

"And what message is that?" Haley asked, looking at Reese.

"That I already have a girlfriend," he said, lifting up her mask and giving her a kiss on the forehead.

Oh my gosh, Haley thought. *I'll so deliver that message to her personally if you want me to, first thing tomorrow morning.*

Haley, cozy in Reese's arms, watched from a distance as Coco and Sasha were reunited at long last.

Sasha lifted her mask to reveal her identity, and at first Coco looked like she might scream and call security. But then her expression softened and she gave her old friend a hug, her eyes misting over. Haley correctly guessed that Coco was only crying tears of relief, over finally having someone to talk to at the party, but she wasn't about to tell Sasha that.

As Johnny patiently waited for Sasha at the table, he tapped out a rhythm for a new Hedon song he was working on. Haley knew his band was currently interviewing guitarists to replace Luke Lawson, and she could tell he felt energized by music again, enough to even sit through a performance of Rubber Dynamite without throwing chairs at the stage.

Reese, meanwhile, had finally stopped squirming in his breeches. Haley snuggled deeper into his arms, as "Rubber D" took the stage in the midst of an impressive pyrotechnic display. Haley suddenly felt, well, proud of herself. She had gotten her guy and had somehow managed to better the fates of those around her. At least for today. And how could a girl ask for more than that?

THE END

Doing the right thing is almost never easy.

Haley had thought of everything while planning Annie's surprise party. She reserved the back room of Lisa's Pizza and ordered a carrot cake—Annie's favorite—from a local bakery. She called all their mutual friends and found at least two Hillsdale students—aside from Dave—who weren't already committed to Coco's bash.

What Haley lacked in peers, she decided to make up for in parents. By inviting the Armstrongs; the Millers, who were planning to bring Mitchell; Mrs.

Metzger; Mr. Von; Ms. Lipsky; Ms. Frick; and Coach Tygert and his wife, Annabelle, to join them at the party.

On the night of the big surprise, Haley wrapped the presents she'd bought for Annie—a pocket Latin dictionary, a cozy for her personal data device, and a guest pass to an upcoming lecture series on "Truth in Memoirs" at Columbia University—in pink polka-dot paper with a white satin bow. She put on her favorite jeans, her blue ballet flats, a white turtleneck sweater and her blue A-line coat and headed over to Lisa's to finish decorating.

"Thanks," Haley said as her mother dropped her off at the pizza place. "See you at nineteen hundred hours."

"I thought you said the Armstrongs were getting here at seven-fifteen," Joan said.

"Exactly. They're bringing Annie. If she sees you in the parking lot, our cover is blown, so you better be on time."

"Okay, okay," said Joan, "but let me get going or I'll never get Mitchell out of the bathtub in time."

"Haley," Sebastian Bodega said when she walked in the door, "what else may we do for help?" He and Dave and Hannah Moss had been filling up helium balloons since five o'clock.

"Thanks again for including me," Hannah said. "When Dave told me how Coco's been treating Annie all these years, I felt it was my civic duty to pull my equipment and engineering skills from the Rubber Dynamite gig." Hannah added guiltily, "I love those guys, but they suck without me."

"Hannah, I can't tell you how much it means to me to hear you say that," Haley said. She turned to Sebastian and kissed him on the cheek. "I know for a fact that Coco invited a certain Spanish stud to her party. You're a sweetheart for blowing it off and coming here instead."

"I do not know what you speak of," Sebastian said, winking at her. "Annie is your friend. And we shall help her celebrate the anniversary of her birth."

It wasn't exactly the ballroom at the local country club, but Lisa's Pizza was starting to look sort of cute, Haley thought. As the others began arriving, she collected the presents and put them on the gift table. At 7:10, she dimmed the lights and hushed the small crowd.

"They're here," she whispered when the Armstrongs pulled into the parking lot. Haley could tell by the look on Annie's face as she walked toward the front door that she hadn't exactly had the best day.

That's all about to change, Annie. Don't you worry, Haley thought, hoping the hastily arranged party would be enough to cheer up her friend.

"We'll have to seat you in the back," a waitress said to the Armstrongs when they asked for a table. "Don't have room for three up front."

"What are you talking about?" Annie asked sullenly. "There are plenty of open tables."

"Annie, don't be rude," Mrs. Armstrong said. "Just do what the nice lady says."

Annie slowly walked toward the back room, and through the double doors as the waitress flicked on the lights. Then Haley and everyone else stood up and yelled, *"Surprise!"* Annie looked stunned.

"Don't look at me," Mrs. Armstrong said. "It was all Haley's idea."

"You did all this? For me?" Annie asked incredulously.

Haley nodded. "Of course. Only I had some help," she said, motioning to Dave, Sebastian and Hannah.

Annie looked somewhat hurt to see Hannah there, but Hannah took the initiative and tried to put her at ease. "Happy birthday, Annie! Wait'll you hear this," she said, flipping a switch. She'd brought her own subwoofers and her MP3 player and had set up a makeshift deejay booth. With the flip of another switch, a disco ball suspended from the ceiling began twirling, casting a rainbow of flickering lights around the room.

"Cool," Annie said, nodding at Hannah.

"Do you like it?" Haley asked.

"Are you kidding? You do realize this is the first real birthday party I've had in seven years, right?" Annie said, her eyes briefly misting over.

"Well, then let's get this party started," Haley said, dragging Annie to the dance floor. "Everyone," she said, getting their attention. "I think we all know why we're gathered here tonight."

"To. Eat. Pizza," said Mitchell in his robot voice. Everyone laughed.

"Yes, that's right, Mitchell. To eat pizza. But also, to celebrate Annie's sweet sixteen. Annie, in the short time I've gotten to know you, you've been a loyal and supportive friend, and I can honestly say that without you, I would probably still be lost somewhere in the math wing at Hillsdale High. So, to Annie. Our lives are better for knowing you. Now eat up, people. We've got hot pepperoni coming at you."

Mrs. Metzger's face went white. "No pepperoni for David," she called out. Haley was momentarily worried that Mr. Metzger might get all *Mommie Dearest* on her, but Mr. Von put his arm around his date and patted her hand, and she seemed to relax.

Haley added, "We've also got plain, organic cheese, and garden-style for the vegetarians in the house."

"Is it really organic?" Joan whispered to Haley.

Haley shook her head no and said, "But don't you dare tell Mrs. Metzger that."

"Annie," Dave said sheepishly after they had each downed a slice, "may I have this dance?"

"Of course," she said. Annie was positively beaming.

Haley watched with great satisfaction as Dave led her to the makeshift dance floor and, in his awkward way, took her in his arms. Moments later, Sebastian was whisking Haley around too, teaching her the tango. As they danced cheek to cheek, Haley looked around the room and realized she was living one of those rare high school moments, the kind that, no matter how old you get, or how far in life you go, you never, ever forget.

THE END

Friends are meant to be trusted, not tested.

Haley waited as Coco patched her into a three-way call with Annie. "Anniekins, it's Coco darling."

"Um, really?" Annie said, clearly surprised to be receiving the call.

"Mmm-hmmm. Listen, I just wanted to let you know I've decided to invite you to my birthday party this year after all."

"Really, wow, that's . . . I mean, I'd love to come."

"But there's a catch," Coco added.

Annie paused. "What's the catch?"

"I'm not inviting your friend, what's her name, that new girl, Haley Miller."

"But why not? Haley's terrific."

"Eh," said Coco. "Those are the rules. Now are you in or out?"

"Can't I at least think about it?" Annie asked.

"In or out, Armstrong? This offer expires in three seconds. Two . . ."

"I don't know!" Annie cried.

"Make up your mind."

"I guess I'm in," Annie said, defeated.

Haley felt a pang of disappointment, but in a way, she understood how tempting Coco's invitation must have been.

"Thought so," said Coco, abruptly hanging up.

Haley then did as Coco had instructed and waited five minutes before calling Annie. *This will be the true test,* Haley thought. *If Annie comes clean, we still have a shot at being friends.*

"Hey," Haley said when Annie picked up the phone.

"Hey," said Annie.

"So have you thought any more about what you'd like to do for your birthday?" Haley asked. "I sort of came up with a list of people we could invite to dinner."

"I'm still on the fence about this whole party

idea," said Annie. "I've gotten so used to not cele-
brating, do I really want to break with tradition this
year?"

"Come on," Haley pressed. "You've got to do
something. You can't just sit home alone on the big
night."

"Well, actually," Annie said, hestitating.

Come on, Annie, stand up for yourself.

"My parents have been talking about taking
me out to dinner, you know, just the three of us,"
said Annie. "Which sounds pretty appealing right
about now."

"You're sure that's what you want to do?" Haley
asked one last time.

"Yeah," Annie said. "I'm sure. So I guess I'll see
you around," she said.

"I guess," said Haley, hanging up the phone.

*After everything I've done for Annie, this is the
thanks I get?* she thought. Mostly, though, she
just felt sorry for the girl. Annie was like a dog
that's treated badly by its owner but doesn't
have enough sense to run away. No matter how
hard Coco hit her, she just kept coming back for
more.

●　●　●

All in all, Haley should have known better than to
put a vulnerable friend in such a tempting situation. If Annie is ever going to break free of Coco's

manipulative grasp, it's going to happen with the support of true friends, not those who dare her to stand up to Coco on her own.

Go back to page 1.

COCO'S SWEET SIXTEEN

Some sixteen-year-olds aren't so sweet.

Haley entered the ballroom of the local country club wearing the cream-colored chiffon dress she'd somehow convinced her mom to buy for her as an early Christmas present. Granted, Haley probably wouldn't have much else under the tree this year, but tonight, it didn't matter. She was just glad to be among the pretty, privileged guests at Coco De Clerq's birthday party.

It looks like Dr. Zhivago *meets* Charlie and the Chocolate Factory, Haley thought, marveling at the over-the-top décor.

The De Clerqs had transformed the ballroom into a winter wonderland, with ice sculptures, dozens of elaborately decorated cakes, a white chocolate fondue station and sixteen custom flavors of ice cream, all in shades of champagne and winter white—Coco's signature birthday colors.

Too bad Coco isn't going to eat any of it, Haley thought, looking at what must have been billions of calories.

High above, three chandeliers were draped with winter white ribbons. On the tables, there were hurricane lanterns with candles, centerpieces of white roses, and place settings of china, crystal and sterling silver.

You'd think Coco was getting married, Haley concluded, making her way through the crowd of chardonnay-swilling adults. She walked toward the stage, where most of the kids were congregating.

Haley knew that Coco had booked Rubber Dynamite specifically to get back at Sasha for dating Johnny Lane, lead singer of Hillsdale's other popular band, the Hedon. Whereas the Hedon modeled themselves on the seventies-era garage rock sound and played all their own instruments and wrote their own songs, Rubber Dynamite was formed in the spirit of eighties new wave. There were only three members—two keyboardists and a lead singer—and usually they just did a lot of inspired covers. Music purists dismissed them categorically. But then, with Coco De Clerq behind them, those "poseur" complaints hardly cut into their fan base.

Maurice De Clerq, Coco's father, banged a spoon against his champagne glass. "Everybody, can I have your attention," he said. "We'd like to thank all our gorgeous friends for coming out to the club tonight to celebrate our Cookie's sweet sixteen." He paused and added, "Not that anyone minds a little free champagne." The crowd chuckled. Mr. De Clerq looked around. "Where's my Cookie?"

Coco joined him onstage. "Light of my life, sixteen years ago tonight, you came into this world and made me the happiest man alive. And even though it doesn't seem possible, every day since, you've made me just a little bit happier, just a little bit prouder and—look around, people—a whole lot lighter in my wallet." The crowd chuckled again. "Mommy and I love you, Cookie. You're our dessert, every day."

"Thank you, Daddy," Coco said, taking the mike and flashing her perfect smile for the crowd. "I'd also like to thank everyone for coming out tonight. Birthdays are a time for commemorating all the years we've been together and all the memories we've shared, and that, friends, is why you're all here tonight. You each mean something special to me. Whitney, Haley, Cecily, you're my girls. Now have fun, enjoy the band and let's get this party started!"

At that moment, Haley caught sight of Ali De Clerq blatantly mimicking her sister at the bar. Ali downed a glass of champagne and immediately ordered another. Haley thought she might need to intervene and made her way over to where Ali was standing. Well, make that just barely standing.

"If it makes you feel any better," Haley said to Ali, "I think about ninety percent of the people here see right through her too."

"Maybe," Ali said, "but Mommy and Daddy De Clerq don't. They think their sugary sweet little cup of Coco can do no wrong. Can you imagine what it's like growing up with that? And she's my baby sister."

"Listen," Haley said, "I've got a younger brother who eats paste and talks to himself, and my parents think he's secretly *brilliant*. You don't have to tell me about favoritism in the family."

Ali sighed. "From the moment she was born, she's gotten everything she's ever wanted." She paused. "Except one thing. Reese Highland. You know he didn't even show up tonight? Which proves that there are still a few things in life your parents can't buy for you."

"Ladies," said Spencer. "You're both looking ravishing."

"I need to be ravished," said Ali. "Take me to the pool house."

"Hello to you, too," said Spencer, as Ali shoved her tongue down his throat.

A waiter walked around ringing the dinner bell, and Haley left the "happy" couple to find her table. "Catch you two later," she said.

Haley was mildly disappointed to hear from Ali

that Reese Highland wouldn't be making an appearance at the party, but then she spotted Matt Graham.

"You look thirsty," he said. "Don't you know that the only way to get through one of these club events is to keep your liver quenched?"

"Tell me you're at table nineteen," Haley said, looking around at the little old ladies filling up the seats at her table.

"Put it this way," said Matt, "wherever you're seated, I'm just to your left." He picked up the name tag from the place setting next to hers, crumpled it into a ball and put his own name tag in front of the plate. "That way I can keep refilling your glass," he said, pulling a silver flask out of his pocket and refilling her club soda glass with vodka.

"Oh, what the heck," Haley said. "It's a birthday party. We might as well have a little fun." She downed it in one gulp.

What wasn't fun, however, was the tremendous headache Haley woke up with the next morning. And the flashes of memories that visited her throughout the day.

Haley remembered, for instance, falling on the dance floor in front of Mr. and Mrs. Highland. Twice. She remembered, unfortunately, pulling up her dress and urinating on the country club lawn on her way to the taxi. She also recalled hooking up with Matt Graham in the cab on the way home, a makeout session that was interrupted when Haley had to ask the driver to pull over so that she could puke. And last, but certainly not least, she remembered her parents' faces as she waltzed through the door an hour past curfew, in her brand-new but now torn and stained dress.

That last mental image was something Haley Miller would not soon forget. And neither would Joan or Perry. As in, it earned her housebound restriction until after New Year's Eve.

THE END

Talking trash will earn you the worst kind of karma.

H: I can't believe Cecily would
   betray me like that.
C: Aren't you pissed?
H: If you want my opinion, she's
   the one stalking Reese
   Highland. Have you seen
   the way she throws herself
   at him?
C: Absolutely. Do you think she'd
   give him her V-card if he
   asked for it?

H: She is a cheerleader.

C: You do know they've already
hooked up? She showed up at
his house last Saturday . . .

H: The little slut!

C: And did everything but. . . .
Reese was the one who put
on the brakes. He said
he wants to take
things slow.

H: I cannot believe I confided in
her. And she was going after
Reese the whole time!

C: So what exactly did you
tell her?

H: You know.

C: I want to hear it
from you.

H: That I was having all those
dreams about Reese.

C: What kind of dreams?

H: You know, where he's all
sweaty, I'm in my nightgown.

C: That's hot.

H: Well, not anymore! They can
have each other!

C: Sorry, babe, I've got to
take this phone call.
Mañana!

H: Later. I've got a dartboard

```
    to build, with Cecily's face
    on it!
```

● ● ●

Since when is bad-mouthing a friend a good idea? Unfortunately, Coco cut and pasted excerpts of Haley's
text into a blank e-mail document and forwarded it to
Cecily with a note explaining how Haley had been talking behind her back for weeks.

Even more unfortunate: Cecily never even blabbed
to Coco. Coco had simply seen how much time the two
girls were spending together and figured Haley must
have confided something juicy to her by that point. So
she'd gone on a fishing expedition. And trolled right into
Haley's embarrassing little secret.

Coco also informed Reese about Haley's sex dreams,
and things between them, as you can imagine, got pretty
weird. Pretty soon, Haley's dreams were the only place
she was seeing him.

Hang your head and go back to page 1.

Either you live and you learn, or you live and get burned.

Haley stopped typing and leaned back in her chair, taking a moment to analyze Coco's message.

Cecily is one of the nicest people I've met at Hillsdale. I really don't think she would betray me. Haley decided to send her an instant message, to check out Coco's story.

```
H: Cecily, u there?
CW: Haley! What's up?
H: Meet me in our usual chat
```

room? Coco wants to ask you
    something.
CW: Sure.

Cecily entered the live chat room.

CW: Hi, Coco! Didn't know you'd
    be here.
H: Coco, I took the liberty of
    inviting Cecily to join us, so
    we can get to the bottom of
    this once and for all.
C: Sorry ladies, I've got to run.
    Ciao!

And as quickly as she'd signed on, Coco De Clerq
disappeared into cyberspace.

CW: What was that all about?
H: Just Coco, as usual, trying to
    sabotage another friendship.
    Here, read this.

Haley cut and pasted Coco's instant message into
an e-mail to Cecily as proof.

CW: What a liar! I can't believe
    she did that. For the record,
    I do not have a crush on Reese

```
     Highland. And I would NEVER
     tell your secrets.
H: Wait a sec. Getting an
   invitation to chat from . . .
```

The screen flashed Reese Highland's name.

```
H: It's Reese!
```

Haley typed, keeping both chat boxes alive at the same time.

```
H: Hi, Reese.
CW: What does he want?
H: Come on! A girl never chats
   and tells!
R: I was just wondering if
   you were going to Coco's
   sweet 16 . . . ?
```

Haley frowned.

```
H: He just wants to know if I'm
   going to Coco's birthday
   party. Ugh. I certainly
   don't want to, after that
   little stunt she just
   pulled.
CW: Seriously. I'm thinking of
```

skipping too. You know, I've
actually been kissing up to
her lately because I've found
that's the only way she gets
bored with you and leaves
you alone. Otherwise, you
end up being part of her
tribe for the rest of high
school. And I couldn't take
that!

H: That's brilliant! Why didn't I
think of that?

Haley responded to Reese.

H: Actually, I don't think I am
going to Coco's party.
R: Really? Me neither.

"No way!" Haley said out loud. She typed:

H: Cool.
R: So, then, maybe we
should . . .

Cecily interjected across the screen.

CW: Okay, I'm leaving you two
lovebirds on your own. Good
luck. Later.

Haley waited patiently for Reese to finish asking her out. *I've waited four months,* she thought. *What's a few more minutes?*

R: Do you want to go out to dinner with me?

So finally Reese Highland was stepping up.

You know, if I were more like Coco, Haley thought, *I would cut and paste* this *chat and e-mail it to her and rub it in that Reese picked me.*

Fortunately, she had more sense than that.

● ● ●

If you think Haley's response to Reese's invitation should be "Yes!!!" turn to DATE WITH REESE on page 241. If you still want Haley to go to COCO'S SWEET SIXTEEN, turn to page 262. Finally, you can pay Coco back for all her tricks and SABOTAGE COCO'S SWEET SIXTEEN on page 213.

LIZ RUCKDESCHEL was raised in Hillsdale, New Jersey, where *What If . . .* is set. She graduated from Brown University with a degree in religious studies and worked in set design in the film industry before turning her attention toward writing. Liz lives in Los Angeles.

SARA JAMES has covered the media for *Women's Wear Daily,* has been a special projects producer for *The Charlie Rose Show,* and has written about fashion for *InStyle* magazine. Sara graduated from the University of North Carolina at Chapel Hill with a degree in English literature. She grew up in Cape Hatteras, North Carolina, where her parents have owned a surf shop since 1973.

Haley still needs your help!

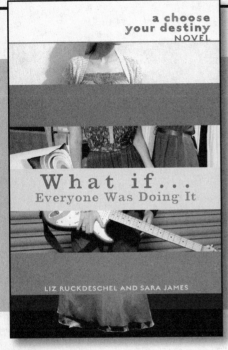

a choose
your destiny
NOVEL

What if...
Everyone Was Doing It

LIZ RUCKDESCHEL AND SARA JAMES

It's prom season and Haley has a lot of decisions to make! Fill in the blanks below to guess what's going to happen in *What if . . . Everyone Was Doing It.*

Sophomore year is ending, and Haley is facing some big _____. Prom is _____. And, after prom, there's even more _____. Will Haley play _____ with Reese, _____ with Spence, or _____ with Devon? Summer is coming on fast, and with it comes a whole bunch of _____. Will the decisions she made all year come back and _____ everything?

www.randomhouse.com/teens RHCB Delacorte Press